Scents of Submission

Lucy Fairbourne

A Male Chastity Femdom Fantasy

VELLUMINOUS

Published by Velluminous Press
www.velluminous.com

Copyright ©2019 Velluminous Press

ISBN: 978-1-905605-53-8

1.0

Scents of Submission

Table of Contents

Scents of Submission 1

Epilogue 103

More Information 105

Scents of Submission

The vintage convertible sedan pulled into the mansion's broad parking area with a crunch of tires on wet gravel. Rain streamed down the car's windows and drummed lightly on the stretched fabric of its roof. The elegantly-uniformed chauffeuse turned off the wipers but left the engine idling; she'd be heading straight back to the local railway station, to pick up a piece of luggage that hadn't fitted into the car.

Of course it was Alex who had volunteered to leave his modest belongings in the care of the station master, in favor of Miranda's three large cases. Even that was barely enough, she'd told him, for a week-long house party with varied entertainments. And anyway, she'd teasingly asked, what was the point of a girl bringing a big, strong boyfriend along on a trip unless she had plenty of luggage for him to carry?

Alex didn't mind. He was ready to put up with most things, as long as they benefited Miranda. He wanted his elegant girlfriend to be able to enjoy her sexy outfits, her high-heeled shoes, her perfumes and cosmetics — and whatever else she needed. If that meant sacrifices on his part, so be it. He found a perverse pleasure in arrangements that outsiders would have seen as unfair.

So, he hoped, did Miranda.

He was smart enough to know that she had other options, a lot more than he did ... and she was strong-willed as well as feminine; uncompromising, focused on her own self-interest. That was the kind of girl she was. If she'd been otherwise, he probably wouldn't have fallen for her so hard.

Alex was painfully aware that, as much as Miranda liked him, she hadn't fallen for him in quite the same way. She made all the right noises but it wasn't the same for her. He tried to persuade himself that it didn't matter. He was here, wasn't he? Arriving in a vintage car, to spend a week of luxurious decadence with the girl of his dreams?

Miranda eased herself closer to him on the leather seat, tilting her head so that her long dark curls tumbled against his shoulder. Alex breathed in, enjoying his girlfriend's subtle fragrance, then glanced down to admire her stocking-covered legs, and how elegantly she arranged her shapely calves and stiletto shoes in the available space. He moved to open his door, meaning to go around to let her out, but she restrained him with a brief caress of her gloved fingers on his woolen jacket sleeve.

"Wait," she murmured. "Someone will be along with an umbrella in a moment, to show us into the house."

"Sounds good," Alex said. The rain was driving down in torrential sheets and if he got soaked now, he'd stay that way until his luggage arrived. "Although, 'house' isn't really a big enough word, is it?" He spent a moment considering the residence where they'd come to stay. "Ancestral pile? Stately home?"

Miranda chuckled. "You'll get used to it after a while."

Alex doubted he ever would. It was too far removed from his own experience: a sprawling mansion, surrounded by its own pastures and woodlands, with a generous scattering of cottages, stables, barns and workshops. Looking at the mansion's stone facade made him imagine elegantly-dressed ladies and gentlemen from earlier centuries, arriving in their horse-drawn carriages and open-topped motor cars for the shooting parties and society balls that must once have been held here.

In the twenty-first century, you had to be almost unbelievably wealthy, to actually live in a place like this ... to maintain it as a working English country estate. You had to be someone like their hostess, a senior partner at the private merchant bank where Miranda was building her career. Alex's girlfriend was tight-lipped with details, but he did know that the secretive firm dated from the Italian Renaissance and had somehow avoided the fate of its peers, most of which had been felled by financial catastrophe or absorbed into the modern world of takeovers and global branding.

Alex and Miranda had been dating for months before he even got a glimpse of her workplace. The nearby pub where they usually met up was being refurbished, so she'd reluctantly agreed that he might wait for her on the premises. He'd been expecting a corporate reception area; what he found was more of a Victorian gentleman's club. Chesterfield sofas; polished brass reading lamps; glass-fronted cabinets filled with leather-bound volumes; antique oil paintings. There had even been a side table filled with crystal decanters.

All of that seemed strange enough, but what struck him even more forcefully was how female-dominated it seemed to be. One of the two receptionists had been male, as had the security guard. After a few minutes Alex had seen one guy who looked like a caretaker ... and that had been it. Everyone else who he saw leaving the premises at the end of that work day had been a smartly-dressed female. Many of them had glanced at him so curiously that he wondered if he might be the first man ever to have sat in their luxurious lobby.

"You know, I'd consider a job here, if it would help with the gender balance," he'd said when his girlfriend emerged from the antique-looking elevator. He was only half-joking: a job in finance would pay much better than the computer-related odds-and-ends he picked up from local businesses. He glanced at Miranda to see how she was taking the suggestion. "You've often said I need to explore new horizons."

She'd shrugged. "The bank is owned and managed by women. Our female clients expect things to be a certain way."

"What about your male clients?"

"Our financial products and services are aimed exclusively at women," she said.

"Can any of your colleagues hack computers as well as I can?"

"The bank employs programmers and security analysts, not hackers," she said primly. "The idea is to keep our clients' information private, not to bring in people who love cracking things wide open."

Alex could have tried to present himself as a "white hat" hacker who'd work to protect his employers instead of harming them, but Miranda's tone had been clear: seeking a tech job at the bank was hopeless. He'd known that, really, even before he introduced the subject.

He decided to try a different tack:

"Well, how many people here can speak five foreign languages?" The idea of breaking into the world of banking was getting more appealing. "Maybe there's some freelance translation I could do? Working from home? If I can put one financial client on my résumé, I might get more…"

He was exaggerating his linguistic skills, but only slightly. He'd learned German at school, then later he'd worked closely with several Eastern Europeans who were starting a game company. That added Czech, Polish and a smattering of Russian to his language list. Being part-raised by a Hungarian grandmother had given him a solid if rusty grounding in that language, too.

"I'm sorry, Alex. Our translation needs are handled internally," she said. "You wouldn't even be considered. But there are a few deserving males in … subordinate positions." She gave him a wicked grin and he felt the familiar jolt of pleasure her knowing glance always elicited. "Service-oriented," she continued, "No résumé required. As soon as we're alone, I'll take you through the job application process."

They were in a public place now so he did his best to ignore the first stirrings of arousal.

Outside the building, as they strolled hand-in-hand, she'd told him of the party. "We're both invited. Come and meet some of our decision makers … I think you'll enjoy them." She paused. "I'm sure they'll enjoy you."

"Really?"

"Of course. A couple of the senior partners have been asking when they'd get to meet you."

"I'm surprised they know I exist," he said.

Miranda shrugged. "Why wouldn't they? I socialize with them. We talk about our lives … about the things that make us happy."

"Like the men who fall under your spell," he said in a teasing tone. "Or how did you put it just now? 'Males in subordinate positions'?"

"Well—"

"Hey, it's okay!" Alex laughed. "Feel free to introduce me as your astoundingly handsome boyfriend whenever you like."

He meant that seriously even if his tone was playful. Miranda might be a rising star among the bank's deal-makers, but her next career step — being offered an associate partnership — was about more than professional skill and commitment. Partners needed to fit in socially, too. It was important for Miranda to participate in high-end corporate gatherings, and crucial for her to bring the right sort of companion.

Alex didn't mind helping advance his girlfriend's career, even if it seemed a little one sided. An entrée into the world of high finance would have been welcome, if only she'd been prepared to throw some contacts his way. Still, he could find his own work … more interesting work too, if not as well-paid.

Anyway, this week-long event was about much more than just supporting her career. Kink had been promised. Miranda was interested in kink. So was Alex.

Kink was the real reason they were here.

*

The rain lashed down even harder as two people emerged from the house: a teenaged boy and girl, Alex thought. Old enough to greet guests, unload luggage, maybe even park a few cars, but a year or two away from being ready to join the party.

Then, as the pair drew closer, he realized that he'd judged too soon. He might have two or three years on the girl, while the guy actually seemed older. What was it about them, he wondered, that had persuaded him they were both so much younger than his own twenty-three years?

He decided it was probably the strange way they were dressed. Up-close he could see that their costumes were of some silk-like material, and completely unsuited to this autumnal weather — a skimpy white tunic for the girl, draped loosely from her shoulders and gathered about her slender waist. The fabric was sheer, clinging so wetly to her breasts and hips that it concealed almost nothing. The man wore a loose, white, rain-spattered shirt, open at the neck and tucked into black pants. No buttons, lacings or zippers were anywhere in evidence, so that Alex had the impression that a quick tug might allow any of these garments to fall open, and perhaps to slip off entirely.

The girl's slim neck was encircled by an elegant-looking choker, adorned with a silver pendant ring that rested between prominent collarbones. The man wore a heavier collar, thick enough for several D-shaped shackle points to be set into the leather itself; more masculine, more businesslike.

Alex turned to Miranda. "Did we miss a memo about this being fancy dress?"

She just smiled at him. "Whatever we're supposed to have will be provided."

The boy and girl approached. Each held a furled umbrella but neither made any effort to use it for their own shelter. Instead they came straight to the car — the boy on Miranda's side, the girl at Alex's — and then opened the passenger doors. The umbrellas sprang up like a pair of graceful twins, perfectly timed to offer shelter to the emerging guests.

The green-eyed girl who ushered Alex toward the house was as petite as Alex was tall, so that he kept wanting to take the umbrella and shelter her instead. He resisted the urge to do so. She looked stunning, even with her blonde hair plastered wetly to her head. Her scent was alluring, too; so faint that he barely registered it, no more than a hint of something wholesome and sweet. Perhaps it was her natural fragrance, Alex thought, accentuated by the clean country rain that soaked her to the skin. He found himself becoming aroused, and half-wished that circumstances might permit him to test his clothes-tugging idea on that clinging shift.

A glance toward his companion showed him that Miranda was regarding him knowingly. "It's okay," she said. "We're libertines for a week, and you're free to appreciate everything that's on offer. I'll even check if she's available later, if you want ... though you might want to hold off on deciding until you've seen the rest of the menu."

They reached the shelter of the stone-columned portico that led to the mansion's imposing front door. The umbrellas were shaken then furled, and the rain-soaked servants stood aside to await the next guests. A young man beckoned them to an outdoors reception area hidden behind rain-damp screens. Miranda presented her left hand without being asked, and he waved a scanner over it.

"Welcome back, madam." The young man touched a tablet computer that rested on a small table. "I have your usual room available, if that's acceptable?"

"Perfect," Miranda replied. "Now, could you fix up my boyfriend? I've already submitted his details."

The man nodded. "Of course, madam." He turned to Alex. "Are you right handed, sir? Then I'll need your left hand."

Alex complied, wondering what it could be about. Then he winced at the sight of the large syringe the man was preparing. He glanced at Miranda. "What the—?"

"It's nothing to worry about," she said. "A chip. It will allow access to the facilities of the house—room service, things like that." She smiled. "The security system is based on these things so I'm afraid it's not optional."

"I guess it's okay," Alex said reluctantly.

When the procedure was complete, he gingerly touched the puncture mark. It felt like a grain of rice under his skin. This was turning out to be weirder than he'd expected.

"Come on, Alex," Miranda said. Her eagerness seemed slightly over-done. "Let's go inside and get the weekend started."

Another young woman welcomed them into the oak-paneled entrance hall. Alex glanced at her as she handed Miranda a mask. He reached out instinctively to receive one of his own, then dropped his hand in embarrassment.

Maybe these disguises were only provided for female guests.

Where had he seen the girl before? He couldn't place her and there was no time for recollection, because Miranda took his hand and urged him on. Somewhere further inside, a string quartet played a Mozart piece, barely audible at this distance. They passed an open doorway that revealed a book-lined study warmed by a crackling log fire.

"It doesn't seem quite fair," he said, "keeping those two employees outside in the rain when it's so pleasant in here."

"Employees?" Miranda's mask was a shapely scrap of lace so delicately woven and webbed that it hid almost nothing — but as she knotted it behind her head, Alex sensed a subtle change. His girlfriend now seemed more completely dressed than him, leaving him immodestly exposed by comparison. She spent a moment arranging the translucent fabric more comfortably and then continued, "These parties are all about the kink. That's why we're here, so I can take my place among the other Mistresses, with you as my slave."

"Um…"

"When you say, 'Um' like that, it makes me think you might be having second thoughts. Are you?"

"Of course I'm not."

"I'm glad to hear it."

Alex thought for a moment. "Then the boy and girl are guests like us? Submissive ones, playing a role?" He hesitated. "But they can't possibly be getting anything out of standing in the rain like—"

Miranda took his hand. "They're *slaves*, Alex. Real ones. The property of our hostess. Probably being disciplined for some infraction. They are not your concern."

She led him deeper into the house, into what appeared to be a full-sized Regency ball room. The place was filling with elegantly-masked female guests and ... hardly any male ones. Where were the husbands? Was Miranda the only merchant banker who had a boyfriend in tow? At last he spotted one. He caught the other man's eye and the two of them exchanged glances. It was impossible to read the other man's expression though Alex was certain he was uncomfortable as well.

Boys and girls moved around the floor, making themselves available as dancing partners or to fetch drinks. None wore masks; many were dressed in the simple garments that Alex now understood denoted enslavement. The musicians were all female, unmasked, and simply dressed too. Other boys and girls wore nothing above the waist except for the collars that seemed compulsory for their sort; a few had no clothing at all — and apart from their heads, every inch of them was perfectly hairless and smooth.

Here and there angry welts showed on naked skin. Alex shivered deliciously at the thought of those whip-marks being placed: who, he wondered had wielded the lash? How did the victims feel now, with their shame visible for all to see?

Except there seemed to be no shame. Even those forced to display their marked flesh — or denied any clothing at all — didn't seem embarrassed by their status. Perhaps it was because they were uniformly attractive in their nakedness. Or perhaps, Alex thought, this was nothing more than a group of submissive men and women happily living out their personal kinks. The other male guest was practically salivating as his eyes devoured one naked slave girl after another, but the glances of the masked Mistresses seemed cooler: judgmental rather than admiring. Several of them appeared interested in Alex himself, even more so than in the delightful display that surrounded them.

Deep inside, a submissive spark flared and he wished he could change places with one of the slaves. To be stripped naked, forced into servitude, subjected to the judgment of sophisticated, discerning women.

Just for the evening, he thought. To see what it was like.

"Our hostess keeps her chattels thoroughly waxed and plucked," Miranda explained to him when he admired the slaves' meticulous grooming. "Body hair is forbidden to them."

She seemed so familiar with everything. Alex knew she'd stayed at the mansion before and even been on the periphery of a couple of parties, but now he started to wonder what she'd actually got up to on those previous visits. Part of him hated the notion that his girlfriend might ever have indulged in such kinky pleasures without him, though he also felt a *frisson* of excitement about the liberties she might have taken, the scenes she might have played out. Had Miranda chosen a virile boy to enjoy? Favored the lucky lad with the sight of her naked body? Whipped him? Honored his grateful mouth with the privilege of tasting her pussy and licking her clit?

Had she honored the slave's hard cock too?

Alex's own cock seemed to like that idea, judging by how it stirred. Maybe Miranda would take the opportunity perform some of those acts again, forcing him to watch in helpless humiliation as she took her pleasure with another.

Fucked another.

Would that be so bad?

After a moment's reflection he realized that it wouldn't be. The dismay he felt at the thought of his dominant girlfriend being unfaithful, was outweighed by his need to please and to obey her. To suffer and to sacrifice on Miranda's behalf, in complete submission to her will.

The female subject of his fantasy seemed oblivious to his inner erotic turmoil. She lazily signaled a bare-chested, collared slave boy. The young man approached and stood patiently as she whispered to Alex, "Isn't this great?" She turned to the waiter. "I'll have a martini," she growled at him. "Extra dry. And my … companion will have an Islay scotch. Something smoky and preposterously ancient."

Which was just what Alex would have ordered, if she'd bothered to ask him. So, he thought, that's how it's going to be. He felt himself relax a little. As long as things carried on like this, he wouldn't mind. Not at all.

*

The party continued until the early hours and Alex's mind was buzzing by the end of it — with excitement, not fatigue. He'd thought himself moderately familiar with the ways of kink but after tonight he understood himself to be a complete innocent. This, he imagined, was how a celibate monk would feel if plucked from his cloisters and thrust headlong into the carnal world.

He'd seen sadistic partygoers doing things — and compliant boys and girls submitting to things — that he could never have imagined. He'd seen female predators stalking their willing prey, and witnessed the degrading delights that followed. Miranda had stayed close, steering him here and there with her gloved hand on his arm, as if to say to the other huntresses, 'Back off, this one's mine.'

He'd seen their hostess circulating among her guests, her face obscured behind a confection of jeweled feathers, statuesque in high heels, clad in a tightly-laced low-cut bodice and tailored leather skirt that showed off her long legs. In one hand she held a riding crop as though it were a rod of office; the other gripped a light chain that had been polished until it glittered. Tethered to the chain was a slave boy, nude except for his collar and a blindfold. He bore no whip marks, but his naked left buttock had been strikingly tattooed with a Chinese character. The boy stood cowed and trembling as his leash-holder studied Alex for a long, electric moment. Then she came closer; he received a giddying waft of her perfume. Neither exchanged a single word. The woman looked him up and down, nodded a friendly greeting to Miranda, and then moved away. The inked slave shuffled blindly after her, amidst a gentle clinking of silver steel links.

A while later, Alex saw her pass both the chain and the riding crop to a plump female guest dressed in a leather cat-suit. The woman's mask was cat-like too, down to a pair of tufted ears that seemed permanently pricked-up. From what he could see of her features Alex judged her to be Asian.

In return for the slave and riding crop, their hostess received a folded packet that she tucked into the rightmost side of her corset top until it disappeared between her breast and the leather. The cat-woman leaned back against a nearby wall and used the crop to tap the boy on the inside of each knee, one after the other. He spread his legs apart obediently and she dropped one gloved hand to his genitals, cupping cock and balls together as if she wanted to assess them. Alex saw that the gloves' fingers and thumbs were adorned with silver claws. The boy's penis stiffened at her touch, and she smiled.

Then the woman placed her palm on the top of his blindfolded head and urged him to his knees, spreading her own legs as she did so. She guided his hands to a pair of zip fasteners; the slave boy undid them. A tailored leather strip loosened and fell open, offering a glimpse of the woman's dark pubic hair. She flicked the whip across her slave's naked flank. Alex barely had time to observe the first gentle kisses sightlessly applied to the flesh that had just been revealed, before a group of dancers blocked the view.

"I wonder what's in the envelope?" Miranda whispered in his ear. "Madam Fen is supposed to be one of the firm's wealthiest clients … and the cruelest to her slaves, too. She's from China. I suppose she'll need an extra plane ticket now. Maybe she'll order her new slave boy to make the reservation."

Alex still didn't know their hostess's name. "That privilege is for her circle of intimates," Miranda had told him when he asked. "She'll share her name if she decides you're worthy … which I think is likely, considering how she looked at you."

He was mystified by that. It seemed to him that the woman had done little more than glance at him.

He was also mystified at how pleased Miranda sounded, that the 'introduction' had gone smoothly. "If she sends for you," she told him, "it's important to me that you do your best to please her."

"Our hostess might send for *me?*" he asked in surprise.

"Don't pretend you wouldn't welcome it," Miranda said. "I could see the effect she had on you." She gestured at the throng of partygoers and submissives who filled the elegant room. "Anyway, you can't possibly have imagined we'd be spending the whole week together, when there are so many interesting morsels on the menu."

As if to illustrate her point, she beckoned a passing slave boy to bring his tray of champagne flutes. "Kneel," she ordered him, and he sank gracefully to his knees — though his tray remained almost motionless, remaining at a convenient serving height. Her tone grew bored. "You may go," she said, and the youth got to his feet and moved on.

Alex hadn't considered the possibility that he and Miranda might go their separate ways, but he couldn't deny that she was right: being in the masked woman's presence had affected him. His scalp tingled as he thought of her, as if ghostly fingers were busy in his hair. His eyes were still drawn to her as she moved among her other guests — unaccompanied now that she'd given up her chained slave.

"What shall I do if I need to speak to her?" he asked. "I can't just call her, 'You.'"

"Wait until you're spoken to," Miranda said. "But 'Madam' is always acceptable, when addressing a dominant female who you don't know … unless she's indicated that you are of particular interest to her, in which case you are to address her as 'Mistress.'"

"Yes, Mistress," he said impudently.

Miranda laughed.

At last it was time to retire.

*

Elsewhere in the mansion, in the bedroom of Madam Fen...

The newly purchased slave boy couldn't keep himself from trembling ... from fear, not from cold. He'd been hearing rumors of Madam Fen for almost as long as he'd been in the mansion: her rapaciousness, her cruelty. After tonight, he was her property. His jaw still ached from the lengthy use that had been made of it. His tattooed left buttock still stung from its recent encounter with the calligrapher's needle.

Madam Fen took something long and metallic from a drawer, and showed it to him. It was a personal branding iron, made to impress her red hot sigil on whichever body part it touched. She pressed the cold metal to his flesh, covering the dark pigment. "Mistress Dominique is a stickler for detail, isn't she?" she said conversationally. "The character matches perfectly. For the other side, do you think? Or would you like it burned on top of what is there already? Perhaps not. It would be a shame to spoil such a perfect ink job."

He didn't dare reply as she set the branding iron down.

"I intend to chastise you thoroughly, later," she said in a conversational tone. "I must warn you that I take pleasure from such things, in a way that you have perhaps not experienced with Mistress Dominique. The more you suffer, the happier I shall be. The more you plead, the harder I shall strike." She nodded vigorously, as if to confirm her own words. "I shall apply my riding crop to your body ... and also the soles of your feet. Then tomorrow, I shall set you to walking." She regarded her slave with what appeared to be genuine curiosity. "Have you ever been punished in that way?"

He shook his head.

"Something new for you, then. But that's for later. For now, get onto your knees and open your mouth."

The newly-purchased slave boy obeyed. He was still naked, still collared, still leashed by the chain by which his new owner had led him to her chamber. They had passed three beautiful, scantily-clad females in the passages. Every one of them had lowered her eyes as a mark of respect for Madam Fen — and perhaps in sympathy with the plight of their fellow slave — but he'd still burned with the humiliation of being displayed like that.

His buttock burned, too, from the needle that had permanently inscribed his skin. Every party guest and every serving slave would have been able to see that he'd been marked with his owner's name as he served her, lapping at her pussy and breathing her most intimate fragrance until he was dizzy with shame and desire.

Now, it seemed she wanted to enjoy his mouth again...

"Wider!" Madam Fen raised her hand and an instant later, the left side of his face stung under her rebuke. "When I order you to do something," she said, "you will do it properly. Promptly and completely. Do you understand?"

He nodded, opening his mouth as wide as he could.

She slapped him again, stingingly, on the cheek that was still burning from her first blow. "That will stop you from forgetting again," she said. "Do you perhaps need another?"

He wanted to say, "No", but that would have meant closing his mouth so instead he just shook his head as rapidly as possible.

"I think you are wrong," she said with a cruel smile, before applying her palm even more powerfully than before.

Then she pushed her fingers between his wide-parted lips, inserting them so deeply that he gagged. "That's to show that your mouth belongs to me," she said. "Once I have you in my home I'll put whatever I want into it. I'll piss into it, if I like. You will drink nothing but water I've washed in. You will lick my feet. My pussy. I will teach obedience to your tongue, and you will use it to please any part of my body that I choose, as often as I like." She paused. "Maybe I'll force you to spend hours licking my anus … would you *like* to clean out my ass with your tongue?"

The newly-purchased slave didn't dare do anything except to nod.

"You would?" Madam Fen laughed. "You filthy little slave slut." She gripped his tongue between her thumb and forefinger. "Such nasty habits, but it seems clean. Go on, stick it right out so I can inspect it." Her grip was pincer-like, leaving him no choice but to obey. "There. Nice and pink. Healthy. Very suitable for providing personal hygiene services."

At last she let him go, but he was too frightened to risk withdrawing his tongue or closing his mouth. She chuckled. "It seems my suggestion pleases you. If your tongue on my ass feels good to me, if it leaves me feeling tingly and fresh, maybe I'll use you like that twice a day. Perhaps with a mint in your mouth? And you shall use a medicated mouthwash first, to make sure you're clean for me. Are you good with that?"

He nodded his head. He wanted to refuse, but refusal was not allowed. He was a slave. He was property. If he resisted, then at best he'd be beaten until he complied.

At worst he'd be returned to Mistress Dominique, who had no patience with rebellious boys. She'd let him go. And as hard as he expected to have things from now on, as cruelly as his new owner promised to treat him … he couldn't give up his addiction to being owned and valued by a powerful female.

During his time at the mansion, the newly-purchased slave had learned an important lesson about himself: the highest honor he could achieve was to please the woman to whom he'd been assigned. To be used as her pleasure toy. To be punished as her whipping boy.

These would be the purposes of his life, from now on.

This was what he was for.

*

The grand staircase that led up to the guest wing reminded Alex of the continental hotel where he and Miranda had spent their first night together as a couple. What a night that had been! Buried in Alex's suitcase, hidden beneath stacks of neatly-folded clothes, was a length of soft rope. He'd fretted about that rope all day, wondering if he'd have the courage to produce it, fearing that Miranda would be appalled at his kinky advances … or worse, that she'd laugh at them.

He'd undressed — a little too quickly, perhaps, but she didn't seem to mind. Then he'd dug into his suitcase and shyly produced his surprise.

"Would you be willing for me to tie you up?"

Miranda's only answer had been a shake of the head … and Alex cursed himself for acting like an over-eager idiot. If only he'd given her some time to get comfortable, plied her with a glass of wine or two, maybe run a hot bath to relax her…

She extended her hand. Before Alex quite knew what was happening, he'd given her the rope … and then, somehow, he found himself trussed up, bound so expertly to the hotel bed that he could barely even wriggle.

Miranda spent the rest of the evening having her way with him.

What an eye-opener *that* had been!

After that experience, he offered to take charge a couple of times, but it was always obvious that Miranda preferred to be on top — and that Alex was better-suited to playing the role of her obedient slave. The more demands she made of him, the more he found himself enjoying her female power and his own submission.

One memorable night she paddled him with her stinging palm until he whimpered and wriggled under the repeated impacts. Afterward, he checked his burning butt cheeks in the bathroom mirror — and was appalled at how rosy-red they'd become.

But less than twenty-four hours later, he found himself craving another spanking, and hoping that this time the experience would be even more intense.

It didn't take them long to add a riding crop to their bedroom toy box.

Under the playful guidance of that whip, Alex learned to pleasure Miranda with his mouth. He'd assumed he was already a competent pussy-licker, but his girlfriend was never shy about showing him how to do better. In fact, she insisted on it — and Alex worked willingly to improve. He loved her intimate taste, and the mingling of her feminine essence with the fragrance she liked to mist on her intimate parts.

He loved all of that even more, when she forced him into acts of oral worship instead of merely permitting them.

Then came the leisurely lovemaking session when after having enjoyed three climaxes of her own, Miranda had led Alex to the brink of his own release — only to leave him hanging. "I want to save you for tomorrow," she'd said. "Or maybe the next day."

After that, it had been understood that she was entitled to deny his orgasms — and with this life-changing principle established, she moved to ramp up her power even more. All decisions about when and how he'd ejaculate were now permanently out of his hands, and in Miranda's. Most likely, whatever happened *would* be in her hands — or sometimes between her oiled feet — because gradually, almost imperceptibly, intercourse had gone from a frequent to an occasional pleasure.

Then it had turned into a special reward, for special occasions.

Lately it seemed to have stopped altogether.

The same went for the rare, fleeting touch of her mouth and tongue, which had been applied to his cock so lavishly when they were first together.

Not any more. Now those roles were entirely reversed.

His male pride sometimes struggled with his changing status, but a deeper, more primal part of him welcomed it. The more he experienced the intense sensations of being trained, teased, denied and disciplined by this fragrant girl … the more he came to need them.

In this way, and with Miranda's subtle encouragement, he gradually came to see himself as *hers*. Not just in a romantic sense but also as a piece of property that she rightfully owned. This slow change in her boyfriend's nature seemed to suit Miranda just fine.

It suited Alex, too. He understood his own submissive needs. He knew how rare it was for someone like him to find a woman prepared to give him the time of day. So here he was, with a dominant female who accepted him and desired him, who'd invited him to explore their mutual boundaries at this week-long kink party. She was the perfect guide because she'd been here before, attending a couple of risqué weekends in the days before she'd met him — although she claimed to have been shy and inexperienced back then, lacking the self-assurance to really participate.

This time, with a suitable companion on her arm, she'd been very clear that they were both going to have the time of their lives.

Judging by how their first evening had gone so far, Alex decided that his girlfriend had been absolutely right.

*

Their guest suite was amazing. Alex had never seen such opulence. The four-poster bed with its oak uprights and velvet canopy would have dominated most bedrooms, but this chamber was spacious enough to take it. The walls were paneled with dark wood and hung with sensual paintings, mainly on the theme of Greek goddesses and their mortal playthings. The two wardrobes were antiques, as was the large gilt-framed mirror above the mantelpiece. Logs crackled in the open fireplace, promising a cheery end to a rainy autumn day. A large wall-mounted video screen, positioned so it could be viewed from the comfort of the four-poster bed, was the room's sole concession to modernity.

The only downside was that his suitcase still hadn't arrived. Fortunately, their private bathroom was already stocked with every toiletry item either of them could possibly need.

"Don't worry," Miranda said. "I'm sure it will turn up by tomorrow morning. In the meantime, you look very fetching as you are — and you'll find clean underwear in the bathroom." She paused, gave him a suggestive smile. "Why don't you freshen up? Take the time to really scrub yourself under a long, hot shower?"

"If you agree to join me," he replied.

"I'd say yes," she told him regretfully, "but I really like the look of that claw-foot tub. Of course, I'll want to be properly attended while I soak. Go ahead and get yourself ready."

Alex didn't need to be told twice. He went into the bathroom to hunt for a razor and a toothbrush. As Miranda had promised, he also found undergarments — boxer shorts and an undershirt, both made of the smooth, insubstantial material that denoted submission in this house. He'd have preferred his own wardrobe, which distinguished him as a guest rather than a slave ... but it didn't matter. The silken garb would be hidden beneath his outer clothes, to be seen only by Miranda ... and he wasn't worried about *her* viewing him as property.

He undressed, stepped into the shower cubicle, and turned on the hot water.

When he eventually emerged, scrubbed and shaved, dried and dressed, Miranda had opened one of the cabinets and was holding the riding crop she'd found inside. She swished it through the air as though testing the suppleness of the leather. Alex felt his cock stiffening and his buttocks tingling in anticipation.

"Open the door," Miranda ordered.

He obeyed, and — to his delight — in came the stunning green-eyed slave girl who'd greeted him with her umbrella and ushered him from the car to the house.

Next, and somewhat less to his delight, in came a pair of costumed boys.

Miranda glanced at these two as they entered the room. "I want you both naked. Now. Then you're to run me a lovely hot bath."

They hastened to obey.

Alex tried to avert his eyes from the disrobing males, though it was hard to ignore how well-muscled they were. He worked hard at the gym, kept himself lean and toned, but these guys…

He turned to Miranda. "Um, what's happening?"

"Nothing for *you* to worry about." Miranda reached down to squeeze his cock and he stiffened instantly, almost before she'd touched him — partly the effect she had, and partly because he hadn't been allowed to ejaculate for days. "I plan to keep you like this, nice and horny, as long as we're here," she whispered. "I also plan to give you to our hostess while I enjoy these boys. If you play nicely … if I get a good report on you … then I might let you cum inside me after I get you home."

He would scarcely refuse such an offer. Miranda, he knew, was perfectly well-aware of that.

"You're to go with this slave girl," she told him. "She'll deliver you to your audition with your new owner."

"My new owner?"

"For tonight, at least. We're here for a whole week, after all." She kept her fist closed around his rock-hard penis, squeezing and releasing. "I know you like the idea that this is my property," she said. "I can feel how much you like the idea … and I'm free to share my property, no?" She paused as if waiting for him to object, then added, "To keep it, or to give it away to whomever I choose?"

Struggle as he might, Alex couldn't deny that his girlfriend's words turned him on. He couldn't deny that they went straight to the heart of him, into the part of his soul that needed to count itself a woman's slave.

He gave an almost imperceptible nod.

"Good," she said.

At last he found his voice. "But you do mean just for tonight, right?"

Miranda shrugged. "It depends."

"What about these two?"

One of the boys was already naked, disappearing into the bathroom. The other was stepping out of a pair of shorts identical to the ones that had been provided for Alex, who did his best to ignore him.

A slight edge came into Miranda's voice. "I'm free to choose my own company."

"You want them and not me?"

"I want to exchange gifts with our hostess. Tonight you're hers to dispose of, while these are mine."

It took him a moment to digest that idea. "Will I see you tomorrow morning, at least?"

"I suppose your new Mistress *might* allow it — but I certainly won't. Not unless I receive an exemplary report from her." She paused. "So make sure you don't disappoint her ... unless you want to suffer the consequences of disappointing me, too. Go on, slave boy. Be off with you."

Alex bridled at her peremptory tone, which had lost every trace of its usual sexiness. He'd never seen this side of his girlfriend before ... but before he made further argument, he considered where he was. Where she'd brought him. Wasn't it the promise of exploring — of pushing boundaries — that had made this party so appealing in the first place? Hadn't he been fantasizing about something like this, just an hour or two earlier? Shouldn't he be grateful for having such a dominant, desirable girlfriend, skilled at creating an illusion of cruelty and willing to make his most perverse fantasies come true?

If he rebelled now, if he decided her kinky games were too extreme, he was afraid that she'd be done with him.

Maybe she's done with you anyway, a small part of him whispered. *Maybe she really is passing you on to another woman. Maybe that's how she lets her boyfriends go, once she's bored with them.*

His mind flirted with that idea, and he found it turned him on too. Only as a fantasy for his erotic imagination to play with, of course...

No, he told himself sternly. Miranda was role-playing. Demonstrating her dominance, testing his submission...

He needed to please her.

So, after a moment, he nodded obediently and caught the waiting girl's eye. She looked even lovelier, now that she was no longer dripping wet. She inclined her head fractionally and went to the doorway, where she paused and extended one hand. He linked fingers with her, and followed her meekly out of the room.

*

"What's your name?" Alex asked.

"Martuska," the girl replied quietly.

He pondered the unusual name. His grandma had taught him enough of her native culture for him to recognize that Martuska might well come from a Hungarian background, just as he did. He'd seen she was beautiful as soon as she emerged with her umbrella to usher him into the mansion; now there was something else intriguing about her.

Would his ancestral language skills be sufficient to let him introduce himself? He couldn't resist trying: *"A nevem Alex."*

The girl's lips twitched as she stifled a smile. He wondered if he'd committed some grammatical howler … even if he hadn't, his pronunciation would probably raise a chuckle from a native speaker. Still, he decided to push on: there couldn't be any harm in telling a woman that he found her beautiful, could there?

"Szép vagy."

This time, Martuska couldn't keep from laughing. "Maybe I should give you some lessons, Alex," she told him. "But not now. We're not supposed to talk."

"But—"

"Hush! We might be overheard."

Alex felt a little uneasy about how attracted he was to the slave girl. It wasn't like him to go around flirting with women who weren't Miranda, no matter how enchanting he found them … but then again, it was his girlfriend who'd knowingly thrown the two of them together … and it wasn't as if *she* was being loyal to *him*.

She'd summoned two naked slave boys to attend her in her bath…

And Martuska was lovely.

Alex pondered these complexities as the girl led him through a small door and into a corridor he hadn't seen before — a narrow, shabby passage quite unlike those leading to the guest bedrooms. This must originally have been for servants, he thought, for maids and footmen who needed to go about their duties without disturbing their social betters.

The stairway they now descended was mean and cramped, too. The wall paint had flaked to reveal patches of smooth plaster; bare treads creaked underfoot. She led him all the way down to ground level and then one flight further. Once, this would have been called 'Downstairs', where the working heart of the house would have been found: the kitchen, the scullery, the housekeeper's room, and so on.

Not any more. Now it was something else entirely: a place of decadence and pleasure. Martuska brought him to a passage, deeply shadowed at either end but lit elsewhere by candles whose flickering light revealed many erotic paintings and prints.

The girl released his hand. "Go on," she murmured. "If you're ready."

"Ready for what?"

"You'll know when you reach the end of the passage. I'll see you back here when Mistress has finished with you. Unless you wish to leave now?"

He shook his head. He wasn't about to run from this house party, not on his first night. He wasn't going to abandon Miranda, or turn his back on whatever new experiences awaited him here.

He was surprised to realize another motive: Martuska expected him to go on, and he didn't want to disappoint her.

As if in confirmation of this, the slave girl put her hand on the small of his back to gently urge him along the corridor.

He proceeded alone, slowly, uncertainly. What was he getting himself into? What waited at the end of the passage? As he moved through the illuminated central section, he took one of the candles from its holder. A glance behind failed to reveal whether his guide was still there: the shadows where they'd stood together were too deep for him to make anything out.

She was probably gone.

Could he go back himself? He was almost at the end of the corridor now. The pool of light from his candle revealed a door, made of heavy studded oak. A suspended ring of blackened iron, positioned above a large keyhole, served as the door handle.

He glanced at several photographic prints that hung close by. He'd walked past most of the pictures in the corridor without really inspecting them, but one drew his attention now: an art photo of a leather-corseted, short-skirted dominatrix. Her face was masked, her body slender. Naked shoulders and creamy décolletage showed above the neck line of her bodice. Her legs were long and shapely, provocatively bare. A wicked-looking riding crop dangled from the woman's gloved fingers, its tip touching her sculpted ankle. She was applying just enough pressure to flex the supple instrument — as if she wanted to suggest how fearsome it would be when used in earnest.

Her feet were bare inside a pair of steel-spiked stiletto shoes.

Alex couldn't tear his eyes away from those shoes. He had a thing for high heels, an erotic appetite that Miranda had indulged freely at first. Then she'd decided that comfortable footwear was a perk of being in charge. Since then, her collection of stiletto shoes had languished at the bottom of her closet, worn only on special occasions.

How different this woman seemed. There was no hint that the shoes were uncomfortable for her. He felt himself becoming aroused as he gazed at her ankles and feet, felt his cock stirring against the constraining fabric of his pants. How elegant she looked. How perfectly the curved riding crop echoed the feminine lines of her body. How skillfully it had been captured by the photographer, so that every braided detail was present. He shivered as he imagined how the crop might feel on his bare skin, and the stark impressions it would leave.

He instinctively understood that being punished by the woman in the picture, being at the mercy of her whip, would be serious, not playful. Not like Miranda's bedroom games.

Was Alex in for something like that now?

He felt sweat prickling under his clothes. His heart was beating faster. His cock stiffened even as a shiver of fear ran along his spine.

Miranda had sent him here. She was offering him to their hostess.

At this very moment, she was cuckolding him, entertaining that muscular, masculine pair in her bedroom. She'd made no attempt to hide her intentions; she'd even ordered the male slaves to strip naked while Alex was present.

He moved his attention from the dominatrix's riding crop to her face — or rather, to the mask behind which her identity was concealed. He studied it closely and realized that it was the same mask that their hostess had worn earlier, to the party.

It had to be the same woman.

Was she the one who awaited him beyond the oak door?

Could that cruel whip be in her hand even at this moment, slightly flexed and waiting to test him?

Perhaps, he thought. Perhaps it could.

If so, then to open the door, to proceed into the chamber beyond, was to make a choice. This was his moment of truth, his last chance to escape. Once he stepped inside, he would no longer be free.

He felt his heart thumping in his chest.

He opened the door.

*

Mistress Dominique was already feeling the familiar glow, the burn that started deep inside her body and that consumed more and more of her until she quenched it through instigating another's suffering. She'd arrived in her dungeon early. Her viewing of the latest acquisition had been pleasing, but now she needed a more leisurely encounter. And what Dominique needed, she almost always got. She'd sent a message to Miranda's guest suite requesting the pleasure of the new slave's company, then she'd descended to her private domain where she could exercise her female power and extract the slave's submission.

Miranda was a skilled procuress; her judgment was as sound as anyone's. Dominique's brief viewing of the newcomer had done nothing to diminish her confidence in her young protégée.

It might even be worth keeping the boy for a while, Dominique thought. Perhaps for quite a long while, if he proved to be a sound investment.

She entered her luxurious inner apartment, adjacent to the main dungeon, and went into the bedroom where she undressed before a tall mirror. She paused to admire her reflection — still firm, still slender — then padded on bare soles to the dressing table. She used a crystal perfume atomizer to mist her neck, the creases of her elbows, her cleavage and nipples, the tops of her thighs, and finally her feet. The tiny droplets were cool on her skin as they dried, and curiously odorless. She replaced the bottle on her dressing table, then returned to the tall mirror where she clothed herself: silk stockings and garter belt; a boned corset and short skirt both tailored from supple leather; half-fingered, full-length gloves of Italian kidskin; black leather stiletto shoes.

The contents of the scent bottle had been provided by Miranda, using information she'd obtained by trial and error, through weeks of subliminal experimentation. She'd had Alex eating out of her hand even with a dilute formulation — he was naturally submissive, naturally attracted to dominant females; the fragrance merely offered the final nudge needed for true enslavement. Dominique had no doubt that the full-strength version she'd just applied, which was tailored specifically for Alex, would work wonders.

Miranda would go far if she continued like this, Dominique thought. The young woman had already proved herself to be exceptional, while in servitude herself.

One must learn to serve before one can truly command: that was one of the bank's iron rules.

Miranda had done well as a slave girl. She'd worked efficiently for the

21

pleasure of her superiors. A few whippings had been necessary (were always necessary); she had borne them stoically. The marks of those punishments had looked good on her naked body, too.

The life of a slave girl wasn't quite right for her, though. Extending it beyond a few weeks would have been a waste of her talents, her organizational skills, her drive. She could never be mistaken for a natural slave.

And so Dominique had soon shifted her subordinate into a more responsible role, offered her a fast-track to junior partnership in return for a steady flow of valuable boys.

That constant supply was important to the clients who attended Dominique's house parties … stupendously wealthy women who had no real need for cash, who preferred to deal with a bank prepared to pay its dividends in other ways…

Dominique's mind went back to her own mentor, officially retired now but still a guiding presence at the bank. Ilse Dijkstra was a formidable woman who'd steered their organization through a less tolerant time. A kinky party such as this, in the home of a partner, would have been unthinkable in those days. Ilse's favorite memories tended to be of gatherings aboard luxury yachts, far from prying eyes, and of slave auctions held on remote islands. The bank's techniques were not so advanced in those days, either; Ilse would sometimes reminisce about rebellious males jumping overboard and swimming for shore.

Today, the firm was enjoying a golden age by comparison. Everything was permissible. Women could truly have power; men could be truly enslaved. There was no need to hide away on yachts or remote islands.

Dominique herself took much of the credit for that. Years before, a boutique perfume laboratory had fallen into her inexperienced lap as part of a large (and costly, to her employer) bankruptcy case. The lab's market value had been negligible. It had been passed to Dominique for a harmless practice run, to see how she performed.

Several colleagues had advised her to sell it immediately so that whatever it fetched could be set against the bank's losses. "Don't waste your time," they'd said. "Write it off today so you can start chasing the next deal."

Instead, Dominique had racked her brains over squeezing a profit from what she now saw as her own little laboratory. She called a meeting with its staff and discovered with pleasure that most of them were women. Several had turned out to be like-minded — broad-minded, too, once she got to know them.

She'd cut costs, ordered redundancies. Both of the male employees had gone, as well as three females of whom she never felt entirely certain.

The remainder had been fully on board. A couple of them were now partners at the bank.

Together, they'd re-jigged the perfume lab to develop new kinds of scent, unique formulations that would help expand the bank's female client list. Once a submissive man had been matched to the perfect blend that tickled his brain *just so*, he could be manipulated without even being aware of it. Transferred from one female owner to another. Gifted. Sold.

And he would never rebel, never even complain, because he never truly understood what was being done to him … and because deep down, he needed it.

Lately she'd been wondering how long the present arrangements could last. The responsibility weighed heavily on her. The world was changing, so slowly that it barely seemed perceptible but then a rising tide was hard to perceive, too, right up to the point where your feet got wet.

The trick, Ilse Dijkstra had always said, was to arrange to be on higher ground before that happened.

Dominique was in charge of a female-owned bank that dated back to the Italian Renaissance. It was her duty to protect that heritage, to think of the long term.

Everyone who came across her path had to be seen as part of that.

*

Alex went through the entrance and closed the door behind him.

He was in a dungeon, surrounded by rough stone walls, shadowed by dancing candlelight.

This was not a fashionable play dungeon, walled off in some secret corner of a fetishist couple's basement. No, this was the real thing. It wouldn't have looked out of place on the set of a big-budget movie, complete with a crew filming a scene from the Spanish Inquisition.

An iron-bound box stood next to the door, its padlocked lid pierced by a small slot. The center of the chamber was dominated by an X-shaped whipping post. A large cage filled one corner. A brazier stood near the whipping post, warming the stone space with its charcoal glow. An unlit passageway showed several shadowy doors. Whips, chains, gags and manacles hung from various walls; one area was given over to a row of branding irons that dangled from polished steel hooks, above a second brazier. Near them was another doorway — narrow, low, leading to who-knew-where. An inner cell, perhaps?

The small door was stout, currently closed. A long platform stood in the corner next to that doorway, fitted with four buckled loops and a spoked wheel. Alex recognized the device immediately as a torture rack.

A leather clad woman reclined in a wing-backed chair that left her shadowed and mysterious, despite the iron chandelier that hung overhead. Her stockinged legs were extended in front of her, stiletto heels scuffing against the dungeon's flagstones. She toyed with a long riding crop, absently using its tip to make patterns on the dusty floor. A small hand bell rested within easy reach.

The woman shifted in the chair so that the light from one flaring candle fell across her face. She was unmasked now, but a single glance was enough to tell Alex that this was the owner of the house. Miranda's boss. Senior partner at the merchant bank. Their hostess.

Except she wasn't exactly his hostess any more. He wasn't exactly sure how it had happened, but she'd become his Mistress. At least for this evening, possibly for longer.

What if Miranda never wanted him back?

His mind shied away from that. The subject was too big, and his present situation was too ... engrossing.

"I see." The woman's voice was a growl. "Close the door behind you and turn the key in the lock."

He obeyed wordlessly.

"That's good." She paused long enough to leave him feeling a little foolish, then continued, "Take the key from the door. I want you locked in."

Alex hesitated. He was genuinely frightened of what might happen to him, once he'd surrendered any possibility of escape. His eyes flicked to the dungeon walls again, to the instruments of correction and restraint that hung there.

"Do my whips and my chains make you nervous?" the woman asked. "Do *I* make you nervous? Good. A slave *should* be nervous in the presence of his Mistress. But he must also be obedient. You will not go anywhere or do anything except serve me, and you will not depart this chamber until I am satisfied. So you won't need the key. Drop it through the slot, into the padlocked box. Let it go ... along with your freedom."

He steeled himself and pushed the key through the slot, heard it thump against the bottom of the locked box.

"Good. Now I have you where I want you." She paused, regarding him critically. "But why have you taken it on yourself to present my property like this? Why have you granted yourself the dignity of clothing?"

His mind was racing so fast he didn't immediately understand what she wanted.

The woman's voice hardened. "I require you to be naked. I will tolerate no obstruction to my gaze. Or to my whip."

He hurriedly obeyed, stripping off his outer clothes, then the slave garments that he wore underneath.

"That's better," she said. "In future, you are to present yourself naked unless I command you otherwise. Do you understand?"

His mouth was too dry for him to make any verbal reply, but at least he managed to nod.

"Now that you're properly displayed, I can see that Miranda hasn't kept up with your grooming," she said. "Perhaps she meant to leave such decisions to me." She fell into a thoughtful silence, then said sharply: "When disrobed, all of my slaves are expected to be perfectly nude. A slave girl will arrange for you to be depilated."

Alex glanced down at his unruly pubic curls. He tried to imagine how it would feel, to be transformed into one of the naked, hairless boys he'd seen earlier. Would he feel more of a possession? Less of a man? Only slaves would be deprived of any choice in such matters. Perhaps that helped explain how youthful Martuska and her companion had seemed, as they came through the rain to meet the car.

He realized that Mistress Dominique was speaking. "Do you see those collars, on the shelf over there?" she asked. "Those symbols of enslavement? I grant you permission to choose the one you hope to receive from me, to mark you as my absolute chattel, to do with as I will."

Symbols of enslavement. Absolute chattel. To do with as I will.

Alex's cock had already been hard, but those words made it twitch and bob until it slapped him on the belly.

What else could he do, other than to obey? He went to the shelf where he found several leather collars in varying styles: thick, thin, plain, ornate, supple, hard.

The collars were all identical in length. Instead of having a tongue that threaded into an adjustable buckle, the straps were adorned at either end by a pair of smooth steel plates: one bearing a notched prong, the other with a matching slot. There were no keyholes, no hint of any release mechanism; when closed, the two fasteners would unite to form a seamless steel lock. The inner surfaces were studded with polished metal disks, placed so that they would rest snugly against the wearer's neck.

Alex quickly rejected the idea of testing any of the collars for size. His task was to choose the token of his own willing subjugation, not to act as if he were in a fetish boutique.

Anyway, he felt certain that any one of them would have encircled his neck perfectly. The woman who was about to enslave Alex had placed these collars here for *him*. She'd either had them custom made, or selected them from a larger collection.

His measurements could only have come from Miranda. She must have known this would happen…

He looked through the collection and found the one that appealed to him most. It was elegant rather than showy, but strongly made of supple black leather. A polished D-ring, positioned at the front, would allow the wearer to be tethered without hope of escape. The others all had various rings and shackles that seemed similarly secure, but the quality and flexibility of Alex's chosen band seemed to give it even more resilience. Once locked about his neck it would not be coming off, he thought. Not without whatever key this strange device required.

Would Miranda be provided with the key?

It didn't matter. His girlfriend had sent him to serve and her inclination matched his own: he needed to offer himself for enslavement. He needed to surrender every scrap of power, of choice, of free will, then face the consequences of that surrender.

A slave boy locked into this collar, and then leashed and chained, would be completely helpless. Imagining this, Alex shivered as he made his selection, picked it up and held it out.

"Is that the token you hope to wear for me, from now on?" The reclining woman sounded pleased at the selection he'd made. "Bring it here, then. Let me inspect my property. Come into the candle light so I can see my new slave properly."

Alex approached, intensely aware of the woman's gaze and her knowing smile, embarrassed by his own nakedness yet aroused by the fact that it seemed to please her. That was humiliating, too, because there was no hiding his naked body's response: the submissive act of choosing his own collar had turned him on so much that his cock wouldn't subside. If anything, it got harder as he came closer.

He was desperate to know what was in store for him. Would he be returned to his girlfriend, once this woman was done with him or was he expected to serve as a house slave, for the rest of the week?

"Kneel," she commanded. "Adopt the natural position of a slave."

Alex dropped to his knees. His cock bobbed up again and thumped his belly. The same thing happened whenever Miranda ordered him into a submissive pose … except his arousal was even stronger now. His cock was even harder.

How could that be, when he loved and desired his girlfriend so much and knew this woman so little?

She took the collar. The leather felt cold and hard as she used it to claim him. The metallic inserts were chilly against the warmth of his neck; their pressure brought a tingling, hair-raising sensation. Now she'd encircled him fully. His scalp prickled at the touch of her half-gloved fingers at the nape of his neck, where the collar's fastener was located. He could feel the unyielding steel of the closing mechanism, sense the toothed prong sliding smoothly into its slot.

She locked the collar with a decisive click and then said matter-of-factly, "Now you are my property. Now you belong to me."

"Please," he said. "What do you want from me?"

"You are to call me 'Mistress," she commanded. "Or Mistress Dominique, if other dominant females are present. Do you understand?"

"Yes, Mistress."

"Then you may ask your question again. With the proper respect this time."

"Please, Mistress. What do you want from me?"

She gave a slow smile. "I want to use you as fuel for the flames I feel building inside me, and then I want to use you to quench them." She reached out with one long leg, nudging the taut muscles of his abdomen with a wickedly sharp-spiked heel. "I want to be free to hurt you. Like this…" and she illustrated what she meant by that with a spiteful jab that made him wince. "Or more cruelly, if I choose. As cruelly as I like. I want to force you … to fulfill every desire that I have for as long as I require. Do you understand?"

"Yes, Mistress."

"And while I take this from you, I want you to remain chaste. Unspent except at my command. I demand your promise to obey."

Was he really free to agree to these terms? He thought of Miranda again. Hadn't she hinted she'd allow him an orgasm soon?

He began hesitantly. "Mistress, I promised my girlfriend—"

"Your 'girlfriend'," Mistress Dominique said, loading the word with sarcasm, "…has promised you to *me*." She paused. "Do you not understand?" She eyed him as if explaining a concept so simple that even a male should have grasped it by now. "You were her slave, but now she wishes you to serve me. Your desires are irrelevant. Now say it. Show me you understand."

"My desires are irrelevant, Mistress."

"And why are they irrelevant?"

"Because I am your slave, Mistress."

"Is it possible for you to have a girlfriend?"

"No, Mistress."

"Why not?"

"Because I am your slave, Mistress."

"And as my slave, what can I do to you?"

"Whatever you wish, Mistress."

"Good." She looked at him thoughtfully. "You have my permission to desire my body. I could hardly keep you from that, even if I wanted to. You may even hope to pleasure me. But those desires will only be fulfilled at my whim. And my whim might well be to take pleasure in other ways. In cruel and degrading ways that you won't like. Even if you serve me faithfully. But you wear my collar now. So you'll accept all of that, won't you?"

"Yes, Mistress. I'll accept whatever you desire for me."

"And do you desire me?"

"Of course, Mistress."

"That ... pleases me." She edged the hem of her skirt up, revealing an inch of stocking top. "Look at me," she commanded. "Look at what you desire. Gaze upon that which you can never truly possess."

What else could he do? He watched as she edged the skirt up further. The sheer silk accentuated the curve of her toned thighs, and Alex groaned with lust.

"Spread your legs. Let me inspect every part of my property. I want to see what effect I have on you. I want to see how your body responds."

The flagstones were cold and hard on his knees as he obeyed. She placed one stiletto heel against his naked inner thigh, where the skin was most delicate. He watched in fascination, shivering at the piercing sensation as his bare flesh dimpled under that cruel spike. Mistress Dominique's polished black shoe leather gleamed in the candlelight; her steel stiletto glittered.

"I can put these on whatever part of your naked body that I choose," she murmured. "I can press however hard I choose." She exerted more pressure. Her shoe spike dug in, painfully. Alex suppressed a yelp.

"I could pinch the delicate skin of your cock under one of these sharp tips, if I wanted to," she continued. "I could put my full weight on it. I could test them on the exquisite tenderness of your balls, if you offered the slightest sign of rebellion ... or even if you don't. It could be an experiment, to see how much you can take." She paused. "What do you think of that?"

His head was spinning; he realized that his mouth was too dry to answer.

"Cat got your tongue?" Mistress Dominique laughed. "You should see your face right now. You can't believe your good luck." She shook her head sadly. "But this is my good fortune, not yours. You'll learn that soon enough."

She brought her stocking covered leg up, tracing her stiletto shoe along his body: first to his groin, then his belly, then his chest. The moving heel spike left a trail of tingling sparks on his naked flesh, manifested as an angry welt as Alex's vulnerable skin reddened under the pitiless stiletto stroke.

She became a little gentler as she reached his throat, his chin, his lips, but only by a slight degree.

There she paused, holding perfectly still.

Alex realized that he was expected to take the spike into his mouth. Its tip was sharp; it had taken almost no pressure to mark his skin … what would it do to the moist, delicate membranes of his tongue or his cheeks? What if she pushed too hard, moved too violently?

He had no choice but to trust Mistress Dominique, to let her do as she wished. He parted his lips and accepted the stiletto heel into his mouth. At first, the shoe's sole pressed against his nose and between his eyes, but he twisted his head to one side so that the arch of her foot could slide past his cheek instead.

"Good boy," she said encouragingly. "My submissive slave already knows what I want."

What she wanted was to be free to penetrate him more deeply with her heel.

"Lick it," she commanded. "Clean it. Explore the tip with your tongue, feel how tiny the point is. I want you to understand its nature. I want you to understand what a dominant female can do to a naked male, when she's wearing these."

He ran his tongue over the cool steel spike until he'd warmed it. After that, the overwhelming sensation was its metallic taste, and the menace of knife-like edges where the elegant curve of the heel intersected with its tip.

He'd never realized how effectively a pair of steel stiletto spikes might be honed to sharpness, if their owner walked regularly on the slabs of a stone dungeon floor.

"Open your mouth wider. Take it deeper. Show me your tongue. Show me your submission."

He complied and she eased the steel spike further into his mouth, tracing the sharp point along the center of his tongue, toward the back of his throat.

Alex fought to control the gag reflex, heard himself making a strangling, choking noise.

"You're not going to complain, are you?" she asked sweetly. "How can you, when you'd do exactly the same thing to a slave girl, if you had the power. You wouldn't hold back, would you? You wouldn't consider her feelings. You'd just ram yourself into her throat until she choked on you, though you'd be using your cock instead of a stiletto heel. The principle, however, remains the same."

His first instinct was to shake his head, to deny that he'd ever mistreat any female in that way, but he didn't dare move. The spike in his mouth felt too threatening, too wicked, too dangerous. So he held himself perfectly still and simply gazed up at her face, begging wordlessly that she would not harm him.

Mistress Dominique gave a low laugh. "And there's the look I've been waiting to see. Scared. Pleading." She stroked a gloved hand along her calf as if to caress her own foot, but shifted her attentions to his face instead.

Her fingers were bare, exposed by the cut of the long black glove and she brushed them along his forehead. "Sweat," she murmured. She inspected her damp fingertips, then brought them to her mouth and licked them slowly, holding his gaze as she did so. "If you only knew how that turns me on, makes me want to treat you even more cruelly ... so I can see more of that pleading. Taste more of that fear."

Alex's tongue was still busy with her high heel. She hadn't given him permission to stop yet; he knew he must continue until she did.

He knew he must appease his Mistress.

"Use your mouth to pull the shoe off my foot," she commanded.

He gripped it lightly with his teeth and his lips and eased it off her. She offered him the other spike heel. "Lick it first. Make it perfectly clean. Take the stiletto deep. Show me that you understand who your mouth belongs to."

He complied.

"Good. Now pull this one off, too."

He lowered the high heeled shoe to the floor as gently, as smoothly as he could, so that it lay next to its mate.

"Now you may gaze at my stocking-covered feet," she whispered. "You'd like to kiss them, wouldn't you?"

Alex nodded. It was true. He was desperate to kiss them ... even more desperate than he'd been when Miranda played this kind of game with him. "Yes, Mistress. May I kiss them, please?"

"Not yet. Not ever, perhaps. It's up to me. For now, you may touch them. Your hands belong to me as well. Use them to massage me."

He set to work obediently, gripping her right foot and working his fingers beneath her stockinged sole.

"That's right. I like a firm touch. Push your fingers under my arch and press me there, pleasure me there. Run your fingers all the way from my toes to my heel. Now run them back again. Keep pressing. Harder."

Crack!

She'd struck him with her flexible riding crop, reaching over his body to land the blow on his left buttock. If her intention was to sting him into trying even harder to please her then she succeeded, because he redoubled his efforts.

"Don't you *dare* take it easy," she growled, "when I am favoring you with my feet."

Alex made sure he didn't take it easy, constantly aware of the riding crop. It wasn't that the single stroke she'd given him had been intolerable — part of him was already hoping for more — but he wanted to please her. Provoking further blows would mean he'd failed in that.

He must have been doing alright, he thought, because the crop's tip remained resting on the floor as she allowed him to continue. After a while, she commanded him to switch to her other foot. His fingers were getting tired, but he didn't dare ease up — particularly when she said, "Harder," again, in a threatening tone.

"That's better. Press your fingers into my arch and work the tension away," she commanded. "Work until I'm completely relaxed. This is your one small chance of earning my approval instead of my riding crop."

Alex repeated the massage as he'd been instructed. His forearms and hands were quivering with fatigue before she was satisfied but at least he hadn't provoked her into administering a second cut with her crop.

"That was … acceptable," Mistress Dominique told him. He watched, fascinated, as she wriggled her toes inside their silk covering. "Now I'm in the mood to find out what service you can offer my bare feet. Move your hands upwards."

He complied, brushing his fingertips up her legs as lightly as he could, scarcely daring to apply any pressure at all.

She rewarded him with a hint of approval that sent a wave of gratitude and relief through him. "That's right," she whispered. "Gently, lightly. Touch my stocking tops. Loosen the fastenings. Now slowly roll the stocking down."

His fingers trembled with excitement at what he was being commanded, no, *permitted* to do, … and with trepidation in case he did it poorly.

The riding crop bit him again as she flicked it across flesh that still stung from her previous stroke. The blow was no more powerful than the first had been, but his skin was more sensitive now, so this one smarted even more.

He knew that a third flick of the crop, applied to the same area, would really hurt.

And if Mistress Dominique ever used her full strength…

"Did I give you permission to touch my leg?" she demanded with another crack of her whip. "You are to take more care."

Preoccupied by the threat of the riding crop, Alex had scarcely been aware that his fingertips had brushed her upper thigh. Hastily he moved his hands back onto the silk fabric that covered her legs. That, it seemed, was permitted. Safe.

Her flesh was forbidden.

"That's better," Mistress Dominique said. "Keep unrolling my stocking."

He worked carefully to bundle the sheer material down over her knee, over her smooth, silky calves. Then he pulled it off.

"Now the other one. Unroll it. And don't you dare touch my skin."

Crack!

"That was just a reminder. If your fingers stray then I shall do it again, like this."

Crack!

She'd shifted the attentions of her whip to his other buttock, and now he felt the burning welt she'd left there, mirroring the stinging mark she'd left before.

"Unroll my stocking," she commanded. "Pull it off gently. There. Now you can see my bare skin. What do you want to do?"

Alex gazed down at her naked feet, enraptured. It was a moment before he could speak; when he forced himself to do so, he could manage no more than a low, husky whisper: "I want to kiss your feet, Mistress. I want to worship them."

"Then you're a very fortunate slave boy, because that's precisely what I require from you. I want you to begin with my feet, to explore every inch of them with your tongue, to show me how completely you belong to me." She paused, looking at him sternly as if daring him to object to the degradation she now demanded. "I want you to take my toes into your mouth until you gag on them."

Alex set to work hastily, hoping that his eagerness would please her…

Crack!

"Take your time."

Crack!

She flexed her slender ankle to present him with the bottom of her foot. "Work your way along my bare sole toward my heel. Kiss it. Taste it. Worship it. Worship *me*. Show me how much you appreciate me. Show me that your mouth is my property. Prove to me that it exists for my pleasure."

Alex diligently covered the sole of her foot with kisses, lapped at it with his tongue, moistened it with beads of saliva, licked them off again. There was something about the taste of her that made him giddy, that reminded him of what he felt with Miranda … but even more intensely.

As he reached her bare heel, Mistress Dominique flicked him lightly with the crop. "Stop for a moment."

He withdrew and watched as she deliberately planted her bare, spittle-slick foot on the dungeon floor. She ground her sole against the stone, then showed it to him. "You've made me get dirty," she said accusingly. "Do you see that?"

He nodded. "Yes, Mistress. I apologize for being so careless."

"Well, you'd better lick me clean then, hadn't you? Wash my foot with your tongue. Remove and swallow every scrap of dust as you work your way back to my toes again. I want you to lick and suck every one. Lick them clean and suck them hard."

He lapped and gulped until her sole had gone from gritty to smooth and slick again, then set to work on her toes.

"Go deep into the clefts, as far as you can. Show me how much you want to serve me, how much you want to earn a place as my slave. Flick your tongue between them. Faster."

His whole mouth was tiring but he quickened the pace as much as he could.

Crack!

"I said faster."

In desperation he found that final reserve of effort and will to serve that could only be urged from him with the right incentive: his need to appease a cruel female wielding a stinging riding crop…

"That's better. That feels nice." Mistress Dominique allowed him to continue for a while. "Now attend to my other foot. Suck my toes."

Daring greatly because he wasn't sure it would please her, he engulfed her first and second toes between his lips, at the same time.

She appeared to approve. "That's right, two at once." She pushed further into his mouth. "Open wide and take the rest of them. Take as many as you can, as deep as you can. I want to feel your tongue working on the ball of my foot. Stop retreating from me! Hold still. I want to keep pushing until I hear you gag."

He braced himself, opened his mouth as wide as he could, accepted her as deeply as he could.

"You will *not* scratch me with your teeth."

Crack!

"Now worship the rest of my foot. Pleasure it. Do it properly."

Crack!

"Kiss and lick every inch. Take your time. That's better."

Abruptly she withdrew her feet, curling her legs up until her bare heels were resting at the front of her seat. "You can rest for a moment. You've done quite well up to now, so I'll reward you by letting you look at my ankles." She paused, giving him time to admire them. "Do you like them?"

"Yes, Mistress."

"Tell me why."

He drew a deep breath, buying time to gather his thoughts. "They're so slender, Mistress. So shapely. The hollows above your heels are so delicate."

"Put your face there," she commanded. "Between my ankles. Smell the fragrance of my skin."

He obeyed, breathing so deeply that his head swam.

"Now you may kiss them. Each one in turn. Pay attention to those delicate hollows you admired so much." She waited as he attended to her left ankle, then her right. "That feels good."

Knowing the risk he took, but impatient for the prize of her pussy that awaited his mouth if he kept moving upward, he proceeded to kiss between her calves…

Crack!

"Take your time."

He dropped back to her ankles again.

"*Now* you may move upward, slowly, as far as my knees. Kiss all around them. Kiss the soft skin behind them. Make sure you find the sweet spot, the one that makes me shiver."

Crack!

"Not like that. Do it gently. That's better. Now kiss my thighs. Every inch of them. All the way around, outside first … now the inside. I want to feel your warm, wet tongue."

He was closer to the prize now. Much closer. His cock stood at attention, ramrod hard. He could feel pre-cum oozing down, trailing cool over his own thighs as he knelt to attend her.

Was she going to give him an orgasm, later? Or would she simply use his mouth for her own pleasure?

He hoped for an orgasm, but he was desperate for her to use his mouth. Presented with a choice between the two, he would have opted to please his Mistress before himself, a thousand times over.

"That feels nice," she murmured. "Perhaps in a while I'll let you really taste me. Perhaps I'll allow you to treat my pussy right, to eat me like a ripe peach, to lap me up, to swallow me like a good little slave. Do you think you are capable of earning that privilege? To please me as I like to be pleased?"

He didn't dare nod. That would have meant pausing in his efforts to win the prize she now dangled before him.

"You're not going to risk answering, are you?" She chuckled at his dilemma. "Is it worth my time to take an orgasm from you?"

He attempted to bob his head as he continued to serve her.

"Perhaps it might be," she said. "And later, if your mouth is pleasing enough, if your tongue is diligent enough, I might reward you with my riding crop. And I don't mean more of these playful strokes."

Crack!

"…but properly, so that you'll feel it and fear it, so that you'll bear my welts for days."

Alex flinched as the crop stung him again, then controlled himself.

"Your mouth is so ardent, so eager," she murmured. "You may continue. You may approach my shrine."

He worked his way up slowly, eager to reach the prize she'd offered but fearful that impatience would displease his Mistress and provoke another cut of her crop. His masochistic soul would have welcomed that punishment, but his submissive nature hated what it symbolized: a woman's disappointment.

Her pussy looked perfect to him. The naked slave girls he'd seen earlier had all been smooth, with every hint of body hair plucked or depilated away, but Mistress was different. Her pussy was covered in dark curls, neatly defined and sparse enough so he could see the damp flesh below, but sufficient to say, 'This is not owned. This is not to be denuded and displayed for another's pleasure.' He approached closer until he could taste the salt-sweetness of her secret lips, sense the incredible perfume that tickled his mind even as he struggled to be certain there was any scent there at all.

"Closer," she commanded. "But don't kiss me there yet. Let me feel your warm breath. Move around my pussy. Breathe. Kiss me very gently, around the edge. And keep breathing on me."

He complied as best he could … and to his relief, he heard her sighing with pleasure at every one of his warm, gentle exhalations. And for his part, he felt himself tumbling more deeply, more delightfully into thralldom, every time he breathed her in.

Then suddenly, without any warning, she flicked him with the riding crop.

"That's enough of that. Taste me properly. Lick me. Work for my pleasure. Let me feel your tongue on my clit. Make it hard and stiff, so you can touch me with the tip alone. Yes, keep flicking it like that … gently. Like the softest brush. Like a feather. Yes, like that. Keep going like that…"

He heard the whispering sound of the crop cutting the air a fraction of a second before it hit and when it did it left a line of pure flame across his backside.

"Take your time."

Alex kept wanting to speed up, to reach for his Mistress's climax — not because he wanted to get this over, but because he was desperate for an orgasm. And he was beginning to suspect that there would be only one tonight: hers.

But he had to be patient, so he continued with the slow, selfless servitude she demanded of him until…

Crack!

"Lick me faster. Lick me harder"

Mistress Dominique was lashing him more fiercely now, but her strokes were still precise, still landing on the same welts she'd been working all along, so that he flinched at every blow. She was still in complete control.

If his mouth had been free, he would have gasped from the pain. Each cut seemed more cruel than the last. He sensed his Mistress's arousal growing with every blow. He cowered on his knees, wondering how bad it would get … and doing his best to appease her by redoubling his efforts, by pressing his aching mouth to her pussy in complete submission, by flicking his weary tongue ever faster.

He sensed the tension building in her body, heard the crop falling to the floor as her half-gloved fingers twisted into his hair instead. She pulled him close, grinding his face into her pussy, transmitting the demands of her body through the pressure of her hands. Her climax lasted for a long time. Alex continued to worship her, to serve her orally. He kept on lapping at her clit in time with the rhythms she commanded, the rhythms that jolted him at every point where his skin met hers, until he sensed that she was coming down.

When she was at last sated, she pushed him away. She had used him; now she was done with him.

*

It had been a long time since Dominique had been so completely pleased, so thoroughly satisfied, by a slave boy's mouth. Female slaves were different; they understood instinctively what to do with their tongues: whether to be soft or hard; how fast to go; when to move from one spot to another.

Males, however, needed to be trained.

Dominique decided that Miranda had made a good start on this one.

She regarded her new chattel. The slave had evidently enjoyed his servitude; he'd been aroused by it. A line of fluid still oozed from his erect penis, trailing down bare skin almost to his left knee. Some had dripped onto the dungeon floor; she rubbed it idly with her bare toes, then placed her sole on his sticky thigh to wipe that spillage away, too.

She offered him her foot again. "You've got your mess on me," she said. "Clean it off."

She wondered if she'd ever tire of degrading her male slaves. Even now, as she basked in the afterglow of the orgasm she'd taken from this one, it still turned her on.

He licked her foot clean willingly enough. Many slave boys would have rejected their own fluids at first, but this one seemed compliant. She wondered if she'd ever find his limits, the point where he'd balk and need to be driven further by force. Perhaps not, she thought. Perhaps the perfume spray — the almost undetectable stuff with which she'd fragranced her feet and her pussy — was so well-matched to him that he'd be powerless to resist her will.

It seemed that way so far.

But there was another test she wanted to perform, in order to be sure of that.

"Get up," she told him. "I want to see how you move. Walk over to the wall." She pointed, indicating where he was to go.

The slave did as he was told. His cock was still ramrod-straight and clearly visible to her as he moved. It was pleasing enough, as cocks went, but what pleased Mistress Dominique most was to have it exposed. To see a male slave stripped, naked, humiliated, deprived of any right to privacy, proof beyond doubt that he belonged to her.

Hanging from the wall to which she'd sent him was a row of riding crops, each one suspended from its own numbered hook.

"Examine them," she told him. "Touch them … caress them… but only the whipping end. Your end. The handles are forbidden to you."

She gave that same order to every new slave. It should have been obvious, she thought, but males in particular seemed naturally inclined to hold a whip by *her* end.

Hesitantly, the slave moved to the end of the row and began to do as she'd commanded.

"Take each one down in turn," she told him. "Examine them all closely. Press the leather tongues to your lips. Kiss them. Taste them. Sniff them. Touch the shafts to your cheek. Sample each one's unique fragrance." She paused to let her commands sink in. "Decide which you prefer."

She drummed her fingers against the arm of her chair as the boy went about his task. The test was routine; nobody ever made an unexpected choice. But Dominique wouldn't have risen so high — either as a financier, or as a procurer of slaves — if she hadn't paid meticulous attention to detail. One day she'd wish to sell this boy, along with a supply of the fragrance that kept him so helplessly submissive — and her clients were not the kinds of women who tolerated unpleasant surprises.

Each riding crop was labeled; one had been generously sprayed with Miranda's perfume formulation. This was the whip she expected him to choose. If he did, then all would be well. It would mean that the formulation was perfect. The boy would be fully enslaved. He could be cataloged and auctioned whenever Dominique herself tired of him.

If he chose a different whip then things might be different. Less satisfactory, perhaps, though Mistress Dominique hadn't risen to her station without learning to relish challenges, or developing the knack of turning setbacks to her advantage.

She could see the boy trembling as he took the leftmost riding crop down, careful to hold it only by its flexible striking end. He studied it in the candlelight, kissed it, sniffed it, just as he'd been told. She knew it to be brand new, and wasn't surprised that he soon moved on. He inspected another, and another. One held his interest for several seconds, but most were quickly set aside.

Then he came to the one that fascinated him, the one he seemed reluctant to return to its hook.

Mistress Dominique forced herself to appear disinterested. She didn't want to rush him, or to give the slightest hint that she expected him to prefer one particular whip. The slave boy's choice had to be pure, based on his preference rather than his submissive desire to please.

"Well," she asked when he'd replaced the final whip. "Which would you take for your own?"

He went back to touch the riding crop that had entranced him.

"Is this the one you'll use to punish me, Mistress?" The boy's voice quavered a little, as if he were frightened. Or excited. Or maybe both.

Mistress Dominique chuckled. "You should be so lucky." She held out her hand. "Bring it to me. Then you may go."

He brought her the whip and she rang the bell that would summon the waiting slave girl. "Leave your outer garments here," she told him. "You won't need them any more. Take the underclothes with you. Chop, chop."

"Yes, Mistress." Clutching the items she'd permitted him, he hurried to the door.

"A slave girl will let you out," she told him. "Then she'll escort you to the boys' quarters."

The lock clicked. The door opened. He went through.

Alone, she checked the label on the riding crop he'd chosen. It read '319'. That was unexpected. A senior banker didn't make simple transcription errors, but Dominique knew she wouldn't rest easy until she'd double-checked her notes. She went into her private chamber where she unlocked a chest and took out her thick, leather-bound punishment ledger.

She consulted the index, then flicked through the book to find the desired entry.

The page she opened was headed: *'Slave Girl #319 —Martuska Farkas'* below which Dominique had penned some lines: *'Martuska is a blonde Hungarian slave girl with green eyes. Shorter & less voluptuous than considered fashionable among slave girls at present, but with high cheekbones, shapely breasts; narrow & high waist; long legs. Competent P.A. fluent in Hungarian & German. Shows great promise though value may be marred by independent spirit and mischievous nature.'*

A little further down she'd written: *'Identically numbered riding crop to be reserved for this slave girl, who should be <u>thoroughly whipped</u>.'* Dominique's pen nib had splattered ink across the paper as she'd underlined that phrase.

She recalled she'd been quite angry at the time.

The rest of the page was crowded with entries showing how often her disciplinary recommendation had been carried out on the unfortunate female.

Or perhaps not so unfortunate, Dominique thought. She gave a slow smile.

Miranda was one of the bank's top procuresses. She specialized in blending subtle, subliminal scents to captivate her chosen male, turning him into a true slave willing to go far beyond anything he'd originally imagined. Her skill had not deserted her. That was obvious from the boy's willingness to forget his 'girlfriend' as soon as he'd come into Dominique's fragranced presence. There had been no need to coerce him, no difficulty in wooing him away. From his point of view, tonight's transfer to a new Mistress had been completely consensual.

His next transfer would seem consensual, too...

Such was the magic of Miranda's concoctions.

However, Dominique could see that whatever aspect of herself Martuska had left on that riding crop — whether it came from the slave girl's sweat, or from her tears, or even from her arousal — had worked an even more powerful enchantment.

If Martuska's feminine essence captured on a leather whip could affect a slave boy so, how would he respond to the physical presence of the girl herself?

An interesting line of inquiry, Dominique mused to herself. What a fascinating discovery. So ... how can I take advantage of it?

*

Alex was still naked as he re-entered the candle-lit passageway. Martuska waited for him to pass, then kept her gaze on him as she softly closed the door.

For a moment he felt embarrassed, tempted to pull on the undershirt and boxer shorts that he'd brought from the dungeon. Then he decided that being regarded like that, by a girl who looked like that, wasn't so bad after all...

"Shall I take those for you?" she asked.

"Um..."

"I'm the only one who'll see you. Come on."

He acquiesced, accepting the fact that he would go unclothed — and that this slave girl would enjoy seeing him that way. Martuska bundled the silky garments under her left arm, then offered him her right hand.

A pool of flickering illumination fell about her. He already knew that her eyes were green, but he hadn't noticed how bright they were before, or how large. The candle light turned her hair to shimmering gold. He gently took her hand and she led him back along the corridor and up several flights of stairs.

There she showed him to a servant's chamber, cramped and simply furnished, perched high up under the great house's eaves so that its low ceiling angled down, relieved by a single tiny window that jutted from the roof line.

As they entered, he felt his collar loosen. Puzzled, he put his hands to it and the strap came undone so suddenly that he nearly fumbled it onto the floor. Martuska giggled. "We're usually allowed to take them off in our rooms … even if it's only to recharge them overnight."

"They have batteries?" he asked in surprise.

She nodded. "That's how the locks work … and some other things." She showed him the charging device that rested on a small shelf. "Leave it there until morning, and make sure you put it back on before you leave. You don't want to get caught being 'improperly dressed.'"

Alex laid his collar on the device, which immediately showed a red 'Charging' light.

"This corridor is reserved for male slaves," she told him. "The bathroom is two doors further along, on the left. That…" and she pointed at an ancient-looking bell mounted over a modern-looking screen, "… is for when Mistress rings for you. Or one of her guests, if she's offered them that privilege. If you're not in your room, your collar will tingle. Then any screen you approach will show you where you're wanted."

Alex swallowed hard. The ramifications of his new situation — of being electronically tagged like a farm beast or some high-value store merchandise — were coming home to him more fully with every passing minute. "Of course," he said. "That's what the microchip implants are for. Every screen tailors itself to whoever stands in front of it."

Martuska nodded. "Why don't you try it out?"

Alex did so. As he drew closer, a pattern of circling dots appeared, spinning and glowing and fading in the universal computer animation that meant, 'Please Wait.'

The delay seemed unreasonably long. "Um, maybe there's a network problem or something?"

"It … takes longer than it should," Martuska said, and after a few more seconds the circling dots were replaced by…

Alex   *Privilege Level: 0 (Slave Boy)Messages (0/0)*
Current Tasks (0)
Feedback Notes (0/0)
Slave Collar Commands
Floor Plans
Quit

Alex watched with impressed fascination, ruefully rubbing the implantation mark at the base of his left thumb.

"The collars have trackers, too," she told him. "The implants were for guests at first, because they can dress however they like. Then a couple of slaves were caught sneaking around without collars, so Mistress Dominique decided to chip everyone. If your collar is here and your implant shows up somewhere else … well, just don't let that happen."

Alex nodded. "Why did it take so long to recognize me?"

Martuska shrugged. "There was a stink about that. Guests were being inconvenienced, trying to use the screens in their rooms. One of the slave boys assigned to the project was let go. The software manager who brought him here claimed he was an expert but, well … I haven't seen much of *her* since then, either."

Alex's brain was already busy with nerd stuff. "Seems like it shouldn't be too hard to make it work almost instantly."

"Don't mention that to anyone else," the girl advised. "Don't talk about the screens at all, or you might find yourself in the technical team … which is in a completely different part of the house … and if you didn't do well there then they might let *you* go."

Alex felt a warm flush: Martuska didn't want him to go.

"It doesn't matter anyway," she said. "They re-worked the system to remember whoever's been using it … so a guest can step away to pour a drink and then get straight back to her movie. Come back over here."

"Okay." He moved toward her.

"You see?"

Alex nodded. His details were still showing, even though he was several feet away. "So, if you go up to it now…"

Martuska did just that. The spinning circle appeared as soon as she was close enough to be detected, followed in due course by her own personal entry:

Martuska	*Privilege Level: 1 (Slave Girl)*
Messages (0/318)	
Current Tasks (1)	
Feedback Notes (0/145)	
Floor Plans	
Quit	

"So nobody can pretend to be anyone else," Alex said. "That's why they were so insistent about chipping me. Do you have one of these in your room, too?"

"Of course." Martuska fell silent for a moment. "But I can't show you. We slave girls are quartered further along the wing. Males are not allowed there without authorization."

"But you can come here … that's because you're at privilege level one, I suppose."

She nodded. "Female slaves have different duties," she said. "We have to be able to go everywhere. Let me show you."

She selected 'Floor Plans', which brought up a blueprint of the immediate area. "We're here." She pointed, then ran her finger from left to right, indicating the corridor. "The slave girls' quarters are over here; the door unlocks itself for female trackers — and the collars shock us, if we cross forbidden boundaries."

Studying the screen, Alex could see they were in an outlying wing of the rambling house. Even with no locked doors and no unauthorized areas, he doubted that he'd be able to find his previous room — Miranda's room, now. And he doubted whether his girlfriend would welcome him anyway. If she wanted him, she'd have sent for him.

For all he knew, she still had those two slave boys with her. Maybe she was amusing herself with them right now. Maybe she had them in that big four-poster bed, lying on either side of her, pleasuring her with their hands, their mouths, their…

Suddenly he couldn't bear to imagine what she might permit them to do, let alone witness it.

"Try not to think about it," Martuska said.

Alex blinked. "How did you know?"

"I could see it on your face."

"Can we check to see who's in her room?"

"Why torture yourself?" Martuska's smile was sympathetic. "Even if you really wanted to, our privilege level is too low." She paused, looking at him thoughtfully. "It might help you to know that you're not the first man she's procured for Mistress Dominique."

"Procured? No, you're mistaken. Miranda is…" He trailed off uncertainly.

The slave girl's voice became serious. "I can tell you what that woman is *not*, Alex. She's not interested in you. You're a bargaining chip to her. Something to be traded away."

"But why would she do that to me?"

"Why do you think?"

He was quiet for a moment. "I know she's hoping for a junior partnership, so ... the only reason I'm here is ... a lie."

She gave him a long, calculating glance. "Is that what you really think?"

When he didn't answer she continued, "In that case, maybe you should leave. Nobody is forced to stay here ... but the longer you wait, the harder it gets to give this up."

Alex tried to hide his confusion. "Give what up?"

Martuska reached out, brushed her fingers across his pectoral muscles, then ran them gently down to his abs. Her manicured nails tingled and sparked on his naked torso as she raked them gently downward, so that he couldn't help drawing a shuddering, pleasurable breath. His cock sprang back to life so rapidly that the slave girl's descending hand encountered its bobbing tip. She withdrew in sudden surprise, then collected herself with a pleased smile. "You see?"

He felt so overwhelmed that he didn't reply.

"Goodnight, Alex."

The slave girl turned away and left him alone. He stared at the screen from where he stood, reading and re-reading her name and her status, imagining he could see her proceeding along the corridor toward the female quarters. After a while he approached it again and Martuska's details vanished, eventually to be replaced by his own.

All of the options seemed self-explanatory, except for 'Collar Commands', so he tapped the screen to bring up the corresponding information.

> *Each slave collar is fitted with several electrical contacts designed to convert authorized commands into signals applied directly to the slave's skin. Every slave is to respond to these signals as follows:*
>
> *One jolt: The slave is to consult the nearest screen for further instructions.*
> *Two jolts: The slave is to strip naked.*
> *Three jolts: The slave must work faster at the present task.*
> *Four jolts: The slave is to report to the dungeon.*

In the case of constant tingling from one collar contact point, the slave is to move in the direction indicated.

Alex studied the instructions, then tapped to close the list. Usually, he had no difficulty in committing this kind of detail to memory, but right now he felt confused, disoriented. Every collared boy and girl in this house would need to develop an instinctive response to the various tingles and jolts, he thought. There would probably be severe consequences for those who failed to heed these electric commands.

He decided to take another look … but the entry was gone. Now, his screen merely showed:

Alex   *Privilege Level: 0 (Slave Boy)*
Messages (0/0)
Current Tasks (0)
Feedback Notes (0/0)
Floor Plans
Quit

He hadn't noticed any mention of collars on Martuska's screen, either, despite reading the whole thing carefully. Maybe the instructions were a one-time deal. He softly cursed the mansion's technical team for a bunch of incompetents, and headed for bed.

*

Alex awoke soon after dawn, to the soft chiming of his room's bell. Low sunlight slanted through the small window — which made at least one pleasant change from yesterday, he thought. As for the rest, he wasn't so sure. He pushed off his thin blanket, grateful that the autumn hadn't turned cold yet, and rose from the narrow bed.

A servant must have lived in this chamber, long ago. Probably under similar conditions, Alex thought. The upper classes wouldn't have spent a penny more than necessary on the comfort of their underlings.

Neither, it seemed, did modern-day Mistresses.

Without bothering to dress, he padded to the wall display, interested to discover what instructions he'd been sent.

Take breakfast in the servants' hall, then report to the granary yard for general labor duties.

Below this message was a floor plan showing that the servants' hall was at ground level, downstairs from the slave corridor where he'd slept. He swiped for another page of instructions, which showed him how to get to the granary yard.

In a cramped closet built into the space under the sloping roof, he found a shirt, pants and a pair of boots. He put these on and made his way downstairs.

The servants' hall was a long whitewashed space, furnished with several scrubbed tables set together in a row and flanked by rough-and-ready timber benches. The area was already filling up with hungry boys and girls, as simply dressed as Alex was himself. Two of those who'd been naked yesterday were naked still, which made him raise an eyebrow. Others had been allowed to dress. Perhaps the two naked ones were still being disciplined. He tried to imagine how he'd feel, if he'd angered Mistress Dominique enough to earn such a punishment.

Dressed or nude, Alex hadn't reckoned with how embarrassed he'd feel at the prospect of breaking his fast among slaves, as a slave himself. He'd interacted with several of these boys and girls before, of course, even if it was only to take some food or a drink from them. He'd even played his own part, sharing in their servitude in the privacy of Mistress Dominique's dungeon. But that was entertainment, fantasy, performance, theater.

This was like being back-stage.

And so he kept quiet as he eased himself into a gap at the table, helped himself to the bread and cheese and fruit that was on offer, poured himself a glass of water from an earthenware pitcher, and began to eat.

"New boy, are you?" asked the neighbor sitting to his right after a while.

Alex bridled because of the two of them, it was the questioner who was the boy — he looked as if he ought to be sitting in a college lecture hall, instead of at the breakfast table in a slave mansion. There was no point making an issue of it, though.

"That would be me," Alex replied. "I got here last night."

An attractive redhead with milk-white skin regarded him from across the table. He recalled that she'd been beautifully nude during the party but now was clothed and still very fetching. Once or twice he'd seen her glance up from her plate at him, but now she pricked up her ears and regarded him frankly. "I thought it was you."

The boy set down his half-eaten apple. "Mistress must have liked the look of you. The other applicant was sent home without even meeting her. So were the three that came last week."

"The other applicant?" Alex asked.

"You must have noticed him."

The girl added, "He spent most of his time ogling me ... and the other naked females."

"Ah." Alex nodded. "I know the one you mean."

"Did *you* take the opportunity to ogle me at all?" she asked.

"Um..."

The boy laughed. "I dare say his eyes positively devoured you." He bit into his apple again.

The girl flushed. "So … has she sent for you yet?"

"Who?"

"Our Mistress, of course. Who else?"

Alex nodded. "She sent for me."

The boy swallowed and nodded. "And now you're here, which shows she likes you. That means she'll be cruel." He took a long swallow of water. "Which means that, as us poor bastards go, you're one of the lucky ones."

"How do you mean?"

"Someone like me only gets to see Mistress once in a blue moon." He fingered his collar. "My job is to attend to the guests, to keep her friends and clients happy. And to labor on the estate, of course. Mistress can be cruel, but life's more interesting if she likes you." He munched another mouthful. "She doesn't like me."

"Why do you stay here, then?"

The boy shrugged. "You know the answer already, or you wouldn't be here yourself. You're an addict, like the rest of us. Early stages for you, and maybe you think you'll kick it … but you won't."

"No one ever does," the girl put in. "Not even when they're sold to someone like Madam Fen." She adopted a superior tone, as if to remind the two males that their status was even lower than hers. "Slave boys, I mean, of course. I've never heard of a female being sold."

Alex didn't know what to make of any of that, so he kept quiet.

She asked, "What's your work detail?"

"Um, manual labor. In the granary yard, wherever that is."

"Maybe I'll come and help you, if I'm free."

The slave boy chuckled mirthlessly. He set his neatly nibbled apple core on the edge of his plate, drained his water glass, and stood up. "Like I said, you're one of the lucky ones."

"Alex!"

He turned at the sound of his name, to see Martuska standing nearby with a canvas satchel slung over one slim shoulder.

"Come on, or you'll be late."

"You should put some bread and cheese in your pocket for lunch … Alex," the pretty redhead suggested in solicitous tones. "My name is Lara, by the way."

Martuska's green eyes flashed. "He doesn't need bread and cheese."

Alex decided not to take any bread and cheese.

She led him to the granary yard, which was an open space surrounded by stone buildings that must once had stored the estate's crops. A grassy bank led up to a mill pond that once fed a water wheel, now still and silent.

They paused a while to watch a lone slave boy trudging … no, limping, around and around the yard. He wore nothing except for an eyeless leather hood that covered his entire head. His buttocks and the back so his thighs were flushed scarlet as if they'd been burned, except where they were crisscrossed with angry blue and purple stripes.

"Poor guy," Alex said.

"That has to be Jasper," Martuska told him. "I heard he was to be sold last night, at the party."

"I saw it." Now that he knew to look, Alex could make out the Chinese tattoo that marked the boy's left buttock, obscured now by the angry bruises and welts. "How could he take a beating like that?" Alex wondered. "And how does he not bump into anything … and why is he doing that, anyway?"

"As for the beating, he had no choice. He belongs to Madam Fen now. She's the cruelest person I know. She must have thrashed him and then set him to spend the day walking here, led by his collar."

Alex tried to recall the instructions he'd read the previous night. Hadn't there been something about one of the collar contacts tingling, with the slave having to go in that direction? That had to be what Martuska meant about the blindfolded slave boy being led. "I feel sorry for him if this is how Madam Fen chooses to treat him," he murmured.

"I feel more sorry about what he must have suffered last night," Martuska said. "Walking in circles is nothing compared to that."

Alex pictured the moment when the boy's fate had been sealed, when the cat-suited woman had claimed her trembling slave. What had led to the transaction, he wondered … and what would he do if the same thing happened to him?

They left Jasper to his lonely trudging and went into a slate-roofed, whitewashed building that turned out to be the old mill house. The windows were tiny but there was enough light to show that the geared shaft of the water wheel had been disengaged. Instead, the massive grindstones were connected to a kind of treadmill: a cross-wise arrangement of heavy ringed beams that jutted from a central pillar, designed to drive the machinery through an overhead system of axles and cogs. He could see the hopper where grain would be fed in at the top, and the battered metal chute where flour would emerge once the mill stones had done their work.

The place was covered in a fine layer of dust but the smell was wholesome: wheat kernels and milled grain.

"You'll be powering the mill," Martuska told him. "It's hard work."

"You've done it?"

She shook her head. "Not by myself. There were two other girls. It would have been too much for any of us, alone."

He looked at the mass of the machinery and decided it might well be too much for him, as well. "Why not use the water wheel?"

The slave girl shrugged. "They like to exercise us, to keep our bodies sculpted and toned. Also, they enjoy watching their slaves hard at work." She glanced upward and following her gaze, Alex noticed the winking red glow of a surveillance camera.

He spent a moment digesting this. "Who is 'they'?"

"Mistress and her friends, of course."

Alex glanced at the shaft he was expected to turn. "Do I just push it around?"

"I'll need to load the hopper first and then keep it topped up," she said. "And I'll take care of the flour sacks as you fill them. But I've been told that someone else wants to take you through the work you're to do."

"Do you know who?"

She shrugged, and then took a fold of his shirt between her thumb and forefinger. "You should probably get undressed before she arrives."

As she spoke, Alex felt a tingling from his collar, from the metal studs he'd noticed when he chose it. It stopped, then repeated.

"Ouch!" he said, though it hadn't really hurt.

"Two mild jolts?" she asked.

He nodded, trying to recall what he was supposed to do. "Um, that means…"

"It means that whoever is coming, expects to find you naked. It'll be better not to disappoint her."

"Thanks, I remember now," Alex said.

"You'll get it soon enough," she told him. "Shall I take you through it again?"

Alex nodded gratefully.

"If you feel one jolt, you'll find your instructions on the nearest screen. Two jolts means to strip naked. Three means someone thinks you're slacking, so you need to get a move on. Four means, report to the dungeon. Constant tingling from one part of the collar means you should go in that direction."

Before she'd even stopped speaking, Alex sensed three jolts. Some dominant woman was watching, and telling him he was being too slow about getting undressed.

He couldn't have denied the truth of that. He'd been worried about remembering his instructions, and enchanted by the fascinating Martuska ... and still a little embarrassed about disrobing in front of her. He had to tell himself that there was nothing to be embarrassed about: he was property; so was she.

There was also the pleasing fact that Martuska seemed so willing to help him ... and that she'd found his nude body worthy of her female attention, when she'd encouraged him to go unclothed through the mansion on the previous night.

He undressed hurriedly, and they stood close to one another in the semi-darkness of the mill house.

Voices approached: two females, chattering carelessly, laughing at one another's wit.

Not slave girls, then, Alex thought.

"Are you sure we won't be on one of those big screens in the bedrooms?" one voice asked.

"We're guests, Vanessa. We're entitled to privacy. The system doesn't monitor us unless we ask."

Alex glanced up at the camera, whose red indicator faded and went out as he looked. The voices came closer and he recognized that the second speaker was Miranda. Presumably in the company of some new friend.

Not long before, he'd have felt an erotic thrill at his girlfriend's arrival. Now he just felt leaden. A moment later, both visitors had slipped past the mill house's half-open door.

Overhead lights came on as if programmed to welcome the two women. Both were dressed casually, in faded blue jeans and comfortable-looking sneakers. Miranda had found herself an oversized check shirt that Alex had never seen before; she also carried a coil of light chain fitted with a padlock. Vanessa's top was more feminine, scoop-necked and finished with floral embroidery. Some kind of peasant blouse, Alex thought.

Miranda said, "So, this is where our bread comes from. It should taste even better, now that you know a few drops of slave boy sweat have gone into milling the flour."

Vanessa giggled as she looked at Alex and said, "I wouldn't mind seeing this one sweating."

It was as if he wasn't even there. He bridled at that — and also at the timbre of Vanessa's voice, which set his teeth on edge — but of course he didn't show it. She approached to inspect him more closely, and he felt a little calmer.

"He's quite a specimen, isn't he?"

"He certainly is," Miranda said.

"And you presented him to Dominique just yesterday?"

"At the height of the celebration. She was quite taken with him."

"Lucky you."

Miranda smiled. "Everything's worked out just as I hoped."

Alex couldn't resist speaking up. "I need you to know that I love you, Miranda. Please don't—"

She turned to Vanessa. "Did this slave boy just say something?"

Vanessa replied, "I couldn't tell. Who could he have meant to address?" She glanced toward Martuska, who had withdrawn to a respectful distance where she stood with lowered eyes. "That one over there, perhaps?"

Alex tried again. "Mistress—"

"Don't call me that," Miranda snapped. "'Madam' will suffice for Vanessa and myself, or for any other woman who has so little connection with you."

He hung his head resentfully, and said nothing.

Vanessa's voice became gratingly solicitous, as if he were a stupid child in need of clear explanation. "Your 'Mistress' would now be our hostess ... the owner whom you served last night ... until she disposes of you, or transfers you to some other deserving female. Then that new woman will be your Mistress." She turned to Miranda. "There. Do you think he understands now?"

"I really couldn't care less," Miranda said. "Still, procuring him was fun, all things considered. It was sometimes tedious but it had its compensations. So, why not one more time?"

She looped the chain through his collar's attachment ring, and then used this improvised leash to yank him toward the treadmill. "Come on, slave boy. There's flour to be milled, or we might go short of fresh bread. And while you're busy doing that, you can do something else for me too. For old time's sake."

She threaded the chain through an iron ringbolt set on one of the treadmill's beams, pulled it until his face was close to the pitted oak surface, and padlocked him in place. Then she tossed the key onto the floor near the door, far beyond his reach.

"Slave girl!" she called. "Start your work."

Martuska was behind Alex and out of sight, but after a moment he heard a rush of grain pouring into the mill's hopper. She must have been standing by, ready to begin her work at a moment's notice. He recalled that she was responsible for bagging the milled flour, too.

The blonde slave girl would be kept busy, he thought, and the physical labor would be hard for her. He half-wished he had the leisure to observe her slender, scantily-clad grace as she stretched up to pour another scoop of grain, or bent for another flour sack. He'd never have been so crass, of course. He'd have offered to help, or to take over completely if she preferred. Anyway, there was no point in speculating. He had his own task, which was even more onerous than hers.

Miranda had already kicked off her sneakers; now she pulled off her jeans and unbuttoned her shirt. She wore no bra, no panties, no underwear at all. Alex felt his heart beating faster. This could still be nothing more than a game, he thought, part of the kink party. He hadn't really been sold to Mistress Dominique. Miranda was only pretending to have lost interest in him.

She might still be as loving and loyal as she'd ever been...

Except he couldn't forget how she'd traded him for a brace of virile boys, on the night they were supposed to spend together. That wasn't the behavior of a woman who intended to express interest in a particular man. He pictured how the evening must have passed in his former guest suite, after he'd been relegated to his narrow servant's pallet ... Miranda luxuriating in her four-poster bed, in a chamber straight out of a medieval fantasy novel ... the roaring log fire ... two naked male slaves, hard-bodied but submissive, eager to please their Mistress in any way she desired.

Miranda would, Alex suspected, have expressed a great deal of interest in *that*.

He pulled himself back into the moment as she boosted herself onto the beam, then scooted along so that she was directly in front of him. She swung one bare foot over his chain so that she straddled it, with her slim legs dangling to either side of his body and her crotch positioned close to his chin.

A waft of perfume hit him. It wasn't the familiar, subtle fragrance that he'd come to associate with this woman, the female essence that made his cock spring to attention before he was even aware of it. No, her new scent was different. Not unpleasant, exactly, but not what he expected.

Not what he desired.

Could it be some lingering trace of another man's aftershave, he wondered? He thought resentfully of the two slave boys. Had her thighs been scented by their smooth cheeks as they lapped at her pussy?

But no. What Alex smelled now was feminine, faintly floral ... and very subtle indeed. It left him cold. If anyone had asked, then in all honesty he'd have had to say he found it vaguely off-putting.

Not that anyone *would* ask a slave boy for his view on the desirability of the pussy he was expected to eat…

"Go ahead," she said. "I want to feel your tongue on my clit and in my cunt. You know exactly how I like it … though I've never used a boy quite like this before. Start turning the mill."

He began to push, quite hard. The machinery didn't budge by an inch.

"Go on!" she commanded. "Get it up to speed and keep it going as you lick me. I want to feel the vibrations running through my body. I want to feel how hard you're working for my pleasure. I want to smell the sweat coming off you. I want the satisfaction of knowing I've added my weight to the machine you have to turn."

Vanessa stood and watched. "Don't wear the poor slave boy out completely," she said. "Leave some for me."

"This one's got plenty of energy," Miranda told her. "But go and find a nice flexible cane, if you like. Then when you take your turn, I'll make sure there's no slacking."

"Won't our hostess mind us damaging her new property?"

"I know a way," Miranda said.

Vanessa vanished, and Miranda took the chain and jerked his mouth toward her pussy. "It's time to get started, slave boy."

This time he really put his back into it, redoubling the efforts he'd used before. The beam lurched into motion. Machinery rumbled; millstones scraped together. Once he had the thing moving, he lowered his mouth and began to nuzzle and lick Miranda's labia … and immediately noticed a downy presence that told him she was growing out her pussy hair.

She'd always prided herself on being perfectly smooth … and in all her time with Alex she'd never failed to maintain herself like that, not once. He'd gone down on her more times than he could count, and received the kind of compelling, honest feedback that would turn any submissive male into a world-class expert on his Mistress's erogenous secrets … and so he was perfectly placed to detect the tiniest change.

That familiarity also meant he could risk letting his tongue slip into autopilot. Previously, he'd never have dreamed of making such an insubordinate move, but his feelings toward Miranda were changing … had already changed. He'd been at the mansion for nearly twenty four hours, spoken to other slaves, seen and done things he'd never have believed. He'd started out believing … hoping … that her sudden coldness was an erotic game.

Now he was coming to understand what had really happened.

Miranda was done with him.

Even that was a comforting self-deception, he realized. He had to be brutally honest with himself, and accept that she'd had no real interest in him in the first place. Alex had been her instrument, used to curry favor with her boss. Maybe for money, maybe for career advancement … but not for him.

Not in any way for him.

Well, if she was done with him, then he would be done with her. It felt surprisingly good, acknowledging that. Sure, he resented the way she'd misled him … but what was the point of mourning something he'd never had in the first place?

And on the positive side, she'd helped him explore and discover his own nature; she'd introduced him to new ideas that had rocked his world … and then she'd brought him to a house filled with fascinating women: to his new owner Mistress Dominique, who'd arrived to shake the structure he'd thought so strong and secure, just as Miranda detonated the foundations.

To slave buyers like the predatory Madam Fen, who fascinated and frightened Alex in equal measure.

To any number of pretty submissive females like the red-headed Lara, with whom he'd shared breakfast.

And to Martuska.

He managed to catch a glimpse of the green-eyed girl, who was studiously ignoring the activity on the treadmill, concentrating instead on her labors. Could two slaves be happy with one another, he wondered?

Keeping the beam moving took a huge amount of effort and a surprising amount of concentration. Several wooden struts had been bolted to the floor, offering the purchase that bare feet needed if they were not to slip under the weight. Alex found that the only way to gain enough traction was to push firmly against one of these crosspieces, and then to pivot up on his toes as the heavy beam moved away.

But Miranda's position and desires meant that he couldn't see the floor. With every step, he had to hunt for the bracing point … and that meant he wasn't able to pay full attention to his other, more intimate duty.

"You'd better buck your ideas up, slave, unless you want a bad report."

After that, he did his best to focus on stimulating her as she desired. Luckily, the timbers were regularly spaced — a little closer than he'd have chosen because petite slave girls were sometimes harnessed to this machine, but he soon learned where to place his feet. After that, he was able to concentrate on Miranda.

She kept him engaged there for a good while. He heaved at the treadmill and licked her pussy. What little he could glimpse of the world went around and around: part of the courtyard outside the half-open door; the disconnected shaft and cogs of the water wheel; Martuska, sweating lightly as she scooped grain from a trough and lifted it high above her head to pour it into the hopper; a sack slowly puffing out as it filled with flour; clouds of dust forming and settling; Vanessa returning to stand watching, lightly switching her denim-covered leg with the long, whippy cane she'd found.

All the while, the treadmill creaked and the machinery rumbled, and his tongue worked tirelessly.

Miranda was taking longer than usual to cum. Normally she'd be reclining in comfortable idleness, propped up on pillows with her legs splayed across their duvet so that he could kneel between them to perform his act of worship. She usually held a riding crop, too, as much to arouse herself as to offer direction to her slave.

Alex found himself working harder and longer, now. But she got there in the end. Her fingers curled into his hair, pulling him closer as her body tensed and her breath sighed from her lungs. Then she pushed him away.

Afterward, she chose to ride the treadmill for a while, throwing her head back as he pushed her around and around. Perhaps she wanted to forget the betrayal she'd committed, he thought. Perhaps she was trying to recapture the simple, innocent childhood experience of riding a playground carousel.

Then he wondered if Miranda had ever been innocent.

She reached down with both legs, using her bare feet to play with his semi-erect cock, then trying to trap his testicles between the curled toes of one foot and the ball of the other.

"I can't get a proper grip from here," she complained as she failed to capture them for the third time. "It's because you won't stay still, slave. Otherwise I'd squeeze you in a way you'd never forget." She laughed. Then, giving up the attempt, she swung her legs up and dropped gracefully from the beam. "Your turn, Vanessa." She reached between Alex's thighs and batted at his penis. "I think I've broken it," she said when it didn't respond as usual. "I don't think it likes me any more."

"Then let's see if I can fix it." Vanessa handed over the cane she'd found, pulled off her sneakers and jeans, then vaulted onto the moving beam. "I'll have what she had," she demanded. "Put your tongue into it, as well as your back."

"Service my friend properly, or I'll take it out on *your* friend," Miranda said. It took a moment for Alex to understand she meant Martuska. Surely she wouldn't harm an innocent bystander, just to punish him? He glanced at the slave girl, who continued her work unperturbed.

Vanessa settled herself into position and parted her thighs before his face. He lowered his mouth to her pussy, which was unshaven, not even trimmed for neatness — and his cock sprang back to life.

Something about her reminded him of how Miranda had once been. What he sensed now was far from identical; Alex could have told with closed eyes that he was pleasuring a different woman, but that familiar, essential hint of something irresistible was there.

Now that he thought about it, Mistress Dominique had shared the same quality. Even more strongly.

What was it about these women's intimate places, he wondered, that made him so eager to be enslaved by them? It wasn't just their pussies; the same thing happened when he got close to their feet, their thighs, their armpits, their breasts. The quality was surely innate, an essential part of each female's individual nature. But if that were true, why had Miranda's fragrance changed? His earlier theory was probably correct, he decided: one or both of the slave boys had left their scent on her.

Or perhaps the change was purely in his mind, driven by his resentment...

Thwack!

Something stung the sole of his right foot and he realized that his cuckolding girlfriend had used the cane on him. It seemed that since she wasn't allowed to make obvious marks on him, she'd chosen this way instead.

It didn't hurt too badly, but then the first blow never did. He began to work more hastily, trying to unlock the secret ways of Vanessa's pussy with his questing tongue. The woman had been using both hands to steady herself on the beam at first, but now she placed one the back of his head, curling her fingers through his hair, guiding him and grinding him as she desired.

Thwack!

Miranda unleashed another wicked stroke, hitting the same spot as before. This second blow really stung. Now the skin of his sole felt as if it were glowing, and he knew it would worsen: each blow would burn hotter than the last. That was how Miranda liked to urge him to greater efforts. The only way to appease her was to please her.

Right now, that meant making Vanessa come.

Thwack!
Thwack!
Thwack!

Miranda wasn't standing still any more, waiting for him to circle and return. Instead she was keeping pace, treading lightly around the treadmill as he labored at the beam. Now she could deliver another stroke every time he pressed the ball of his foot against the next wooden strut, every time he exposed his naked upturned sole.

The mill turned so slowly that she had plenty of time to skip ahead of him, to set up the next assault.

Thwack!

Thwack!

Thwack!

"Hit him harder," Vanessa gasped. "Slave boy, I want you to lick me faster every time she hits you. Then slow down. Keep hitting him, Miranda. I want to hear the snap of the cane. I want to feel how responsive his mouth can be. I want this slave to suffer … so I can get there."

Thwack!

Alex pointed his tongue and lapped it hard and fast over her clit … and then slowed down.

Thwack!

He did it again…

Thwack!

… and again…

Thwack!

… and to his relief, the sadistic woman began to come.

Miranda stood back until her friend was done. Then Vanessa released Alex's head and pulled herself away from him. He kept pushing, turning the treadmill, still carrying her around with him, happy to be free of that punishing cane.

As he bent himself to push the beam even harder, he felt his cock slapping against his belly. He hadn't had any attention to spare, until just now, to realize just how turned on he'd been by Vanessa's fragrance, and by his submissive attention to her pleasure.

Perhaps, even, by the stinging of the cane.

Then…

Thwack!

Thwack!

Thwack!

"Those last three were my goodbye present, slave boy," Miranda said. "So … goodbye!" She glanced at Martuska. "Keep it up, slave girl. The hopper needs to be well-filled so this beast of burden can build his muscles and earn his keep. Come on, Vanessa, we've been promised freshly-baked bread with lunch!"

The two women dressed themselves and left without a backward glance.

Alex kept pushing the treadmill; Martuska kept feeding grain and bagging flour. Neither said a word. After a while, the overhead lights faded and the camera's red indicator began to wink again.

*

"It's time for us to stop for lunch," Martuska told him around noon. "You need to keep your strength up or you won't last the day."

He allowed the treadmill to trundle to a stop; the mill house fell suddenly silent. Martuska's dusty sandals barely disturbed the quiet as she retrieved the padlock key from where Miranda had carelessly tossed it. She approached to release Alex's padlock and he felt his scalp tingling as his leather collar shifted against his neck. She'd been sweating but she still smelled good to him. He was almost disappointed when the padlock opened, the chain slipped away, and he had no reason to stand so close to her any more.

The girl was so beautiful…

He became aware that he was responding to that. Willingly, purely from her proximity, not because he was being compelled through enslavement to worship her body … though now that he thought of it, he knew he'd have no objections to that.

Alex realized that he'd been keeping his weight on the balls of his feet, to save his smarting heels and soles. He sensed Martuska's attention on him as the slave girl took in his pose. "Should I put my clothes and my boots back on?" he asked shyly.

"Is it too painful for you to stay barefoot?"

"Well, that cane did hurt quite a bit … but no."

"Then … is it that you don't like being naked with me?"

"Of course not. I don't mind that at all. It's just that…" He glanced down at himself.

Martuska smiled. "It's flattering. To know you're having an effect on some-one you like."

"In that case, I'll stay naked for you."

"I'll get to see you even more naked soon." She unbuckled the satchel she'd brought. "Mistress has booked you in for depilation."

He considered that. "All of it?"

"All of it," she confirmed. "It's what's appropriate for a slave." She began to remove their packed lunch from its bag: several foil-wrapped portions of

58

chicken, plus tomatoes, bread, cheese and fruit. "It might be more pleasant to eat outside, but at least no one will notice us in here."

"Miranda and Vanessa noticed us," he observed. "And the camera has come back on."

"Miranda had a reason to be interested in you, and to show off for Vanessa."

"They're … lovers?"

Martuska shrugged. "Not as far as I know. Vanessa is a new bank client. Miranda is showing her the ropes."

Alex resisted the temptation to add "… and the chains." Partly because it would have been a poor joke; mostly because it seemed a bit too close to home. Instead he said, "I'm glad I met her, in spite of everything. I'd never have … found my way here, otherwise."

Martuska gave him a knowing glance. "I'm glad too."

He bit into a drumstick and raised an eyebrow in appreciation. "This is better than I expected. The bread, too. Delicious."

She gave a mischievous smile. "I helped make packed lunches for some guests going on a day trip. They won't miss a few pieces of chicken. As for the bread … after our work today, we're entitled to sample the end result."

Alex was instantly worried about what would happen if Martuska got caught. "Please don't get in trouble," he said.

She just laughed. "I'm almost always in trouble."

A few pieces of chicken were left over at the end of the meal. "You should take them," Martuska said. "There aren't many opportunities to eat well here, unless you're a guest."

"Will you keep some for yourself?"

She shook her head. "I've had plenty, and you're the one doing the really heavy labor." She went to his clothes and pushed the foil packets into his pockets, then packed everything else away while he went back to work. "You'll be here again tomorrow," she told him. "But I'll have duties elsewhere, so you'll have to operate the mill on your own. You've seen what it involves?"

"Yes." Alex didn't think he'd have any problems repeating the slave girl's tasks; after all, he'd been watching her every opportunity he got. "But why do they need so much flour?"

"You should see the piles of provisions they get through at these parties," Martuska told him. "And a few of the bank's clients like to buy estate produce for themselves. How did Miranda put it? Something about our sweat?"

Alex struggled to remember. "It makes the bread taste even better."

Martuska nodded. "And other foods too, all produced by slave labor and so in demand among … her sort."

They worked together for the rest of the day, and when the final batch was bagged, she declared their labors done. They went outside together, to rinse the dust away at a dilapidated water trough that was fed by a trickle from the old mill pond. Then Alex dressed and they returned to the servant's hall, where a simple evening meal was being served.

Martuska ate quickly and then excused herself, saying she still had several tasks to complete before she could sleep. The poor girl looked exhausted after her long day feeding the machine.

Alex was exhausted too, and ravenous. There wasn't quite enough food, so he was glad to have the chicken to eat later, back in his room. He pushed the foil packets beneath his mattress, in the hope of being able to use them to wrap more scavenged meals in future.

His hunger was now cured but it turned out that his bed must wait: his collar summoned him to the room's screen, which told him to proceed to a wing of the mansion labeled as 'The Spa'. There, in a treatment room, he found himself ruefully undressing before another pretty slave girl (how he wished it could have been Martuska) who applied wax strips followed by fine tweezers to remove every trace of body hair.

He was so tired that he'd certainly have fallen asleep on her couch, if the process had been less painful.

"You're lucky," the girl said conversationally. "Mistress Dominique has asked me to book you in for a more thorough depilation. You'll see the details on your screen over the next few weeks."

Alex looked down at his newly-smooth flesh. "How can it be more thorough than this?"

"This spa offers both laser and electrolysis treatment," she said with every indication of pride.

"But … won't that be permanent?"

She shrugged. "Isn't enslavement permanent?"

"Yes, I suppose it is."

"Mistress and her friends prefer their slaves' skin to be nice and silky to the touch, so that's how we must be." Her smile seemed as innocent as it was dazzling. "Don't you agree?"

Alex nodded. "Yes, yes, of course. You're perfectly right."

"There. You're done for now. Look out for your next appointment, and I'll see you soon."

Back in the slave quarters, he showered and then tumbled into bed …

where he slept the sleep of the slave who's been well-worked and thoroughly plucked.

*

The next work day passed in a similar fashion, except without the distracting presence of Martuska, and without any humiliating visits from sadistic female guests.

Alex had been nervous about that possibility as he arrived at the mill house. As a slave, he was obliged to obey every female guest who wished to use him, to service her in any way she desired. Once, that would have been the kind of sexy scenario Miranda might have spun for him when he was simply a submissive and clueless boyfriend. Her warm, whispering lips would have breathed the idea into his ear, and he'd have been hot and hard and ready to go.

Now that the fantasy had turned into reality, what he yearned for most was to be owned by a single, loyal Mistress.

So he was happy to be left alone with his work. His body still ached from the previous day's labors, but he forced himself to turn the treadmill, to load the hopper every time it emptied, to place empty flour sacks and remove them when they'd been filled. The process went more slowly because he had no help, but also there were no distractions, and the necessity to take breaks from the treadmill meant that he could work faster once he'd returned. There was no friendly female with a 'borrowed' picnic lunch to share, so Alex had taken Lara's advice from the previous day: he'd brought some bread and cheese and an apple from the breakfast table.

As he ate, he found that he missed the slave girl's food.

He missed the girl herself even more.

The day's work was completed before sundown. He looked for Martuska in the servant's hall, hoping she'd be able to join him as he ate, but she wasn't there. Disappointed and exhausted, he made his way upstairs. His collar tingled as he entered his room, so he checked the wall display.

'To relax you after your labors, a hot tub is prepared for you in the slave bathroom.'

Alex couldn't keep himself from grinning like an idiot. A hot bath was just what his weary muscles needed.

*

The slave boys' bathroom was a place of candle-lit, faded gentility. The tub was long and deep by modern standards, but its ancient enamel had chipped and flaked, revealing patches of dark cast iron underneath. The faucets were ornately old-fashioned and long past the point where they could be polished to brightness. The soap dish was an old saucer from the kitchen, while the pitcher that stood next to it was made of cheap enameled tin.

Even so, everything seemed as clean as it could be made, allowing for the cureless shabbiness of so many decades.

The candlelight probably helped.

The floor was of black and white tile, crazed and cracked and with grouting discolored by time. This bathroom might have been installed a century ago, he thought.

Someone had already filled the bath with steaming water. Alex was grateful for that, because when he'd tested the plumbing earlier, the hot faucet had delivered nothing but a slow, lukewarm trickle. A trail of splashes showed where his benefactor had been hauling pails of water; a large puddle showed where most of the spillage had occurred.

He tested the temperature with his hand. It was perfect. Time to undress and get in, he thought.

Just then, there was a knock at the door.

"May I come in?"

Alex's heart began to beat faster. "Of course," he called.

The door opened and Martuska entered. "Thank you." She carried two steaming pails, archaically constructed of iron hoops and wooden staves, and balanced on a long milkmaid's yoke. For a moment Alex pictured Martuska as an eighteenth-century farm wench, and couldn't help smiling.

She lacked any of the traditional milkmaid's garments, though — unless there was a time when such girls would have adorned themselves with towels. Martuska's was cream-colored and plush, wrapped around her body so that it barely concealed her nipples, leaving the sweet upper curves of her breasts delightfully exposed. Alex allowed his gaze to roam downward, and saw that the towel did an even worse job of covering her shapely thighs.

Tucked into the top of the towel was a small bottle.

"I've brought you more hot water," she said. "And some scented bath oils."

Martuska bent over to set down her main burden, giving Alex a delightful view of her pert, cotton-covered rump ... and of several pink welts shining against the pearly skin of her thighs. She pulled out the bottle, uncorked it, and swirled its contents into the tub.

As she did so, the inadequate towel came undone. Alex barely managed to grab it before it could fall into the water.

He'd been wondering if the slave girl had anything on underneath. She didn't. He already knew her body quite well, having seen it revealed by the downpour as he'd arrived at the mansion, and later through observing her at work in the mill house. He knew her curves and angles as though he'd actually caressed them, her long lissome legs and the silk-sculpted outlines of her small breasts. He'd memorized the clinging, cloth-revealed contours of her slender waist, the flare of her hips. Everything about her had seemed perfect to him ... but that was merely a preview. This was the real thing. Martuska's nakedness took his breath away.

She seemed perfectly unaware of the effect she was having on him. He was grateful to be spared that embarrassment, and fretted that his developing hard-on would become obvious to her, once he undressed for his bath. She'd already told him that his virile response flattered her, and he wasn't ashamed of his cock, it was more about his inability to do the slightest thing to manage its behavior.

Miranda had kept him chaste, and Mistress Dominique had been very clear that she required the same thing of him so Alex tended to get hard at the slightest stimulation.

Martuska's presence was very far from being the slightest stimulation...

The slave girl appeared oblivious to any of his turmoil. "Oh well," she said. "Mistress meant the towel for you, anyway. I've been struggling with it for hours. I'm glad to be rid of it, honestly."

"You've been wearing it—?"

"Since this morning," she said. "I'm afraid that I've been in disgrace all day. The towel was part of my punishment."

"At least you had something," Alex said. He was thinking about all the slaves he'd seen who'd been denied any clothing at all.

"I thought so at first," she admitted. "But the towel kept coming untucked, even though Mistress ordered me to keep it on. It's been a real nuisance." She paused thoughtfully. "She can be quite inventive with her punishments."

Alex stood back to avoid crowding her — and also to better appreciate the slave girl's naked beauty. Now he could see that the whip had been applied more thoroughly than he'd noticed before; the whole rear of her body from waist to knee was crisscrossed by angry welts. He flinched as he imagined how much that must have hurt her.

Martuska turned and saw where his gaze had been focused. Her cheeks reddened slightly. "I was slow preparing Mistress's bath this morning. And I didn't warm her towel properly. That's why she sent me to you ... she said I need more practice."

"So this is a kind of punishment for you?"

"Mistress intends it that way."

"It's a reward for me."

"I think she intends that, too," Martuska said. "It's rare for her to send a slave girl to one of her males. But your reward can only go so far."

"That's … a shame."

Alex saw the slave girl's bare shoulders twitched; not quite an indifferent shrug, more a gesture of helplessness. "Not everything can be as we desire." She turned away from him, displaying the welts again. "I didn't desire these marks," she said. "But … do you like them? Or would you prefer my skin to be pure and unmarred?" She hesitated. "Do they spoil me for you?"

Alex considered the matter. "Nothing could spoil you for me. But I'd never want you to be hurt."

Martuska smiled. "Hadn't you better get ready for your bath? I feel a bit lonely, being the only one who's undressed." She came toward him and reached for his shirt. "Here. Let me help you." She eased it off him, then helped him with his pants and his silken shorts. His cock was already erect as it sprang free.

Now he was naked, too.

"You look good like that," she told him.

"Like what?"

"Perfectly nude. I haven't seen you like that before."

He glanced down at himself. The smoothness of his body still surprised him. He'd need some time to get used to how boyish it made him feel.

"Get in the bath," she suggested. "Mistress wants you spotless."

Alex lowered himself into the steaming tub.

She dipped some water into the enamel pitcher and then poured it over him. With her free hand, she picked up the soap and worked it over his back, his shoulders, his chest.

Then she replaced the slippery bar in its saucer and lathered him — gently at first, then more firmly.

It felt good. He hadn't realized how much his muscles ached, until he experienced the relief of her massaging fingers.

The head of Alex's cock made a sudden appearance from under a layer of bubbles, and Martuska giggled.

"I'd better make sure that's clean too…"

He lay back as she reached down and gripped him. Squeezed him. Stroked him.

"That feels good, doesn't it?" she breathed as she continued to work him.

"It feels good to me. Nice and strong and hard in my hand. Let me keep on … washing you, for a while."

She was as good as her word.

Alex heard himself moan.

Martuska asked, "Would you mind if I sat on the edge of the bath, with my legs in the water? These tiles are a little hard…"

"I don't mind," Alex said. "In fact, it's big enough for both of us. Why don't you just join me?"

She declined to go that far, but she perched herself on the side, steadying herself with both hands. One of the girl's bare heels pressed against the enameled iron of the tub as she eased her left foot beneath his thigh. Her right foot reached between his legs, and a wave of pleasure surged through his body as five delightfully slippery, wriggling toes encountered his cock.

"Would you like to touch my leg?" Her toes were on top of his penis now, trapping it. She began to move her foot up and down. "You can, if you like. I want you to touch me. You don't have to wait for permission. Not with me."

Alex needed no more encouragement to put his hand on the dainty ankle that dangled next to him, brushing the outside of his thigh. Her other foot continued to press on his erection, slithering along the shaft in the soapy water.

He moved his hand upward, cupping her slender calf, then even further, inside the taut curve of her thigh.

Martuska sighed with pleasure. "I like how that feels. I like the sensation of your fingertips claiming my skin." She sighed again, then shivered. "It makes me tingle all the way up my spine." She shifted slightly so that she could straddle his cock with two toes, and then began rubbing again. Back, and forward; back, and forward; back, and forward…

Suddenly, she stopped. "Don't let yourself go completely," she warned. "You were about to come."

The only response he could offer was a frustrated groan. His last orgasm seemed so long ago that he could barely remember it…

"I'm sorry," she told him. "I wish it wasn't forbidden. But you need to take a moment."

He forced himself to think of other things. Mundane, non-erotic things that would enable his body to draw back from the brink. Working the treadmill. Putting the flour sacks in place. Unwrapping a piece of stolen picnic chicken. The simple food of the slave hall.

"Good," she murmured. "You're … a little more relaxed now. Still hard, though. I can feel it. Now, let's see how you like this…"

She climbed into the bath and sat opposite him, and then gripped his cock between her slippery bare arches, and began to stroke him like that. Back, and forward; back, and forward; back, and forward…

"Don't come! You mustn't come. Mistress won't be pleased if I use you up."

Alex tried to plead with her to continue but all that came out was a groan. He tried again: "Please!"

Martuska shook her head. "Your release is hers to grant, not mine." She twitched her feet on him again; he jerked with pleasure. Then she continued, "Mistress won't grant it though. Not tonight, maybe not ever. She likes to keep her slave boys frustrated."

"But you don't have to," he managed to say.

"If only it were my choice. I'd love to see you spill yourself … in my hands, or on my feet … or to feel you spurting inside me. But I don't dare." She paused, as if re-thinking that. "*We* don't dare. We'd both be punished most severely if she found out that I'd stolen a pleasure that belongs to her."

"But … all my pleasures belong to her," he said.

She shrugged. "That doesn't mean I can't amuse myself with your cock … and with you. It doesn't mean you can't enjoy me, either … as long as you have the discipline to stop in time."

She pushed herself up onto her knees, making more room in the tub for him. "Why don't you slide down a little?"

As he complied, she parted her thighs to straddle him. "You must learn … discipline. Mistress requires iron self-control in her slaves. I'm going to help teach you."

She was poised over his straining penis now. Slowly, she eased herself down until her pussy kissed the tip of his hard cock … and then a little further.

He marveled at the wetness of her, at how delightfully slippery and tight she was.

She continued until he was almost completely inside her. Then a little further … and then back up, withdrawing herself almost completely. "Can you stay in control if I keep doing this?" She began to move a little faster. "Can you deny yourself long enough for me to come?"

Alex's voice sounded hoarse in his own ears, almost inaudible as he managed to say: "At least one of us should." He couldn't bear to deny the beautiful slave girl. Not least because he knew how much he'd enjoy her climax too…

She slid down on him, engulfing him completely, circling her pelvis so that her pussy ground against his groin. He could feel himself deep inside her. She was telling him how it felt for her, how hard he was, how deeply she was transfixed…

Her long toned legs pumped her body up and down, her pussy up and down. Alex lay back in the water and closed his eyes, because looking at her pushed him towards climax, but he couldn't resist her body … so he opened his eyes again and reached up to cup her breasts.

"Pinch my nipples," she told him. "Hard. I want to feel it."

He did as she asked, squeezing those sensitive nubbins of flesh between thumb and forefinger until she moaned with pleasure. Then he slid his hands down to her hips, gripped her as she rode him.

"Dig your fingers into my welts," she told him. "Hurt me."

He cupped her buttocks, still warm from what had been done to them, and pressed his fingertips into her flesh.

Then she slowed down. She still rode up and down on him, but now she was concentrating on each stroke, relishing each sensation, timing each thrust to match the unfolding rhythm of her desire.

She began to come … and kept coming. He watched her face the whole time: flushed cheeks; half-closed flickering eyes; ecstatic smile. It was if she'd disappeared into some private world of pleasure.

At last she returned.

"Whoooo. That was really nice."

Alex was still gasping from the effort of holding back. He found he could say nothing, do nothing except to continue looking up at her.

"You nearly came, didn't you? You got too close to the edge. You'll need to work on your self-control. But for now … you're still nice and hard … still ready for Mistress."

Next, she reached for the soap and began to wash him again. "I'd better get you squeaky clean," she told him. "Ready for whatever she has in mind."

"She's very lucky, to own someone like you," he told her.

Martuska laughed. "Maybe she'll give me to you."

"I don't think that's how it works," he said.

She shrugged. "Maybe it could, if she decided you were ready to own a slave, instead of being one."

"She'd never … I mean, I'm the wrong sex."

"I suppose you are," she said. "But I think you'd make a good Master. A little too kind, perhaps. But that's better than too cruel. Some of Mistress's friends are very cruel indeed."

That piqued Alex's interest. "Who is the cruelest?"

"Madam Fen," she said without hesitation. "She comes to most of these parties, and as often as not she buys herself a new toy."

"We saw what she did to her latest new toy," Alex said. He was thinking of poor Jasper walking around the courtyard outside the mill house, and remembering how he must have suffered under Madam Fen's lash.

"Jasper was always a little strange," Martuska told him. "I knew him for a while. He needs someone cruel, someone who'll show him no pity." She paused. "You don't, though. With any luck Madam Fen will be busy with Jasper until it's time for her to take him home. Anyway, Mistress Dominique likes you."

"What does that mean," Alex asked.

"It means you're safe for now."

"Well, when will I *not* be safe?"

"On the day when Mistress Dominique grows bored with you … and someone like Madam Fen starts showing an interest instead," Martuska told him.

*

Almost as soon as Martuska left, while Alex was still dressing himself, he received two tingling jolts from his collar. Then there was a pause. Then came four more jolts.

He recalled what the slave girl had told him: two jolts meant he was to strip naked. Four jolts meant he was to report to the dungeon.

Was he in trouble? Had Mistress Dominique somehow discovered what he and Martuska had just been up to? Or was this just a routine summons?

There was only one way to find out. He stripped off the clothes he'd just put on, and hurried towards the slaves' staircase.

The candle-lit dungeon seemed much the same as when he'd left it, except today it felt colder. Also, Mistress Dominique's high-backed chair had disappeared, and the inner door was open. The X-shaped whipping post dominated the room even more powerfully than before, and it was occupied. By Martuska.

The slave girl was still naked. Her wrists were already secured by glittering chains that stretched her slender arms up and out, revealing the naked hollows of her armpits and the taut sweetness of her pert breasts.

Mistress Dominique was busy securing her victim's ankles. Alex felt a wave of dismay mingled with arousal: his cock was stiffening even as he watched.

Another slave girl stood in a shadowy corner, barefoot, scantily clad in a clinging shift, but watching with an air of smugness. Alex spent a moment trying to recall her name: it was Lara, who'd sat opposite him at breakfast on that first morning. Only a couple of days had passed since then, but it seemed like a different life.

"You didn't expect to get away with such a crime, did you, slave boy?" Mistress Dominique asked as she buckled the final ankle strap.

Alex said, "I am to blame, Mistress. It is I who should be punished."

"And you *shall* be punished. But this slave girl was the one who took the lead ... and so she is the one who must suffer first ... and who must suffer most."

He looked at the angry welts that had already been placed across Martuska's naked rump and thighs. She looked so vulnerable, bound to the post. He didn't think she'd be able to bear being whipped again so soon.

"Mistress, please permit me to take her place," he said.

Mistress Dominique regarded him impatiently. "Every extra word you speak without permission, will earn this slave girl another stroke of my whip."

Alex clamped his mouth firmly shut.

"Lara, lock him in the cell and uncover the grating. He may watch from there, in silence."

"Yes, Mistress."

Lara took Alex by the arm and steered him firmly toward the small inner door, then through into whatever lay beyond. He heard the outside bolt sliding home. His new prison was inky dark at first, but before long he heard a panel being removed, allowing a glimmer of light through a small barred window. Now he could see into the dungeon, and also make out his surroundings: a tiny stone cell, presumably intended to hold slaves adjacent to the torture chamber, so that they could witness a punishment or await one.

Or perhaps both. That seemed to be Alex's likely fate.

He gazed through the window. The cell was positioned so that Martuska was side-on to him and facing a little away. Iron candelabra were positioned behind the whipping post, illuminating the prisoner's body and throwing a giant, X-shaped shadow on the opposite wall. It was as if the slave girl had a dark twin, spread-eagled on the stones, bobbing and swaying as if already under the whip.

Alex could see Martuska twisting her head to gaze around the dungeon, taking in the braziers and branding irons, the manacles and chains. She spent a moment staring into a corner that Alex couldn't presently see, the one where the torture rack stood. The girl's flawless features contorted with fear as she contemplated the machine.

How vulnerable she looked, Alex thought. How fragile in the candle light.

How warm and glowing were the highlights on her shoulder blades, standing proudly like two wings; how smoothly their shadows blended into the darkened curve of her spine. How beautiful that flicker and fade would be, playing across such a flawless feminine composition, if only it were a thing in itself and not a prelude.

*

Martuska had not expected to go unpunished. She'd tasted forbidden fruit; Mistress Dominique was no fool. The slave girl had known there would be a price … but she hadn't expected to be brought to this place. She knew her Mistress's dungeon by reputation only. The severe punishments meted out here were usually reserved for boys.

She didn't regret her actions … but she hadn't expected to be this afraid. She tried desperately to cease her trembling, to control her fear, but it could not be controlled.

Despite her nakedness, despite the chilly air, she was perspiring. She could feel the slick sweat of terror forming between her bare breasts. Droplets formed under her armpits, beaded together, ran coldly down her exposed flanks.

Mistress Dominique must have sensed it, because she took Martuska's left wrist and forced her arm upward. The slave girl stood obediently still as half-gloved fingertips pressed into the smooth dampness of her armpit. Then Mistress Dominique brought her fingers to her lips, licking them slowly, taking her time, savoring her slave girl's fear.

Then Martuska found herself being led to the center of that place of punishment.

The whipping post was made of two sturdy oak beams, fastened together in the shape of an X.

It was adjustable, with several handles and levers. But Mistress Dominique didn't need to change a single thing to match Martuska's petite frame … she seemed to know that the slave girl had been destined to be there, the next one chained to this cruel machine. The dominatrix's grip was firm as she secured her slave girl's right wrist to the end of the beam.

Martuska lifted her left wrist up to its shackle without being told, hoping that obedience would earn mercy. She did so despite herself, because she already knew it wouldn't work. Mistress would have her way with her. Even so, it was better to submit meekly, because the slightest hint of defiance would make things much, much worse.

And so she obediently spread her legs, placing her bare feet next to the tethers at the base of the machine. The door opened while Mistress Dominique was busy with the ankle bonds. Martuska twisted her head and saw that Alex was here, his face pale, his eyes wide.

"You didn't expect to get away with such a crime, did you, slave boy?"

"I am to blame, Mistress," Alex said. "It is I who should be punished."

"And you *shall* be punished. But this slave girl was the one who took the lead ... and so she is the one who must suffer first ... and who must suffer most."

A moment passed and then Alex asked to take her punishment upon himself.

Martuska shivered, grateful that the slave boy had tried to help her, yet hoping desperately that he'd now leave it alone.

Mistress Dominique paused, as if she wanted to give him the opportunity to keep arguing, but he made no further reply. "Lara, lock him in the cell and uncover the grating. He may watch from there, in silence."

"Yes, Mistress," Lara said.

Martuska couldn't crane her neck far enough to see where Alex was being taken, but she heard the small door opening and closing, and the scraping sound of a metal panel being removed. Now mortification was added to fear: she would not have wanted Alex to see her like this: fully tethered by wrist and ankle now, completely helpless. Yet it seemed he was to witness everything, hear everything, that Mistress meant to do to her.

She looked around desperately, found herself staring at a device with restraints and a spoked wheel. She hoped it was not a rack. Or that if it was, then it was only meant to impress ... to intimidate.

Not to be used.

Another glance around made her realize that she hoped the same for almost every instrument she could see. That they were not to be used. Not on her.

Please, not on her.

More sweat ran down her naked flanks. The rivulets felt cold and clammy on her skin. The whipping post was cold, too, where it pressed against her vulnerable flesh. She felt herself shivering again.

Mistress Dominique turned a small crank and Martuska felt a leather-padded crosspiece pressing against her lower belly and hips, twisting her already taut shoulders as it thrust her exposed haunches back.

"How inviting that makes you look," Mistress Dominique murmured. "How ... available. But I want you even more vulnerable." She stepped around the whipping post and Martuska trembled again as a length of rough hemp encircled the sensitive skin of her waist. She could feel the rope's harsh texture, how it was constructed, how spitefully the tiny fibers prickled against her nakedness.

How was she to endure the whipping she knew must soon follow if this everyday sensation alone affected her so?

Mistress Dominique hauled on the rope so hard that the whipping post creaked. Martuska heard herself gasping from the surprise of it. Woven strands sawed against the timber frame, then cinched cruelly about her waist. The pressure was irresistible, pulling Martuska's midriff forward and twisting her tethered arms back from her shoulders. Now, her limbs were spread-eagled across the X-shaped frame and her body was arched between its upper members, as if to depict an angel of suffering.

Anyone seeing her like this, would instantly have known that her naked rump was being presented as a sacrifice to the whip. They might also have wondered if the slave girl's helplessly-outthrust breasts were being offered, too.

Proprietary fingertips traced a path down Martuska's right hip; then they moved on to caress her bare buttock. "Securely bound and prepared for punishment," Mistress Dominique whispered. "Can you still move your limbs?"

Martuska shook her head because she couldn't, not by a single inch.

Surely, she thought, her Mistress must be done with her preparations now. Surely the whipping would begin. Let it begin soon and end soon, she prayed silently. The sooner it began, the sooner it would end.

But Mistress Dominique was not done. Not yet.

At her signal, Lara came to stand behind Martuska, who felt the other slave girl beginning to plait her long blonde hair, gathering the tresses from the crown of her head. Lara's fingers were gentle and skilled, sending pleasurable jolts down Martuska's arched spine and across her tingling scalp. As the redhead finished her task, she deftly wove something in the last few inches of Martuska's long plait, something that bumped ponderously against the small of her back.

The naked girl shivered as Lara pressed the heavy object against her exposed spine, just for an instant. It felt like a cold steel ring.

Lara's silken shift rustled as she padded back to her shadowy corner. Mistress Dominique returned to the whipping post. A moment later, Martuska's world went completely dark. She'd been blindfolded: robbed of sight as well as freedom.

Something hard and cold touched her lips. She knew better than to resist, so she opened her mouth obediently to accept it. Her lips and tongue soon told her that it was a sphere, formed of cold metal and so large that she could barely take it in. Mistress Dominique pushed it deeper, until Martuska had to struggle to keep herself from gagging. Her closing lips encountered the tightly curved metal rod to which the ball was attached.

She realized that Mistress Dominique had put the bulbous end of a smooth steel hook into her mouth. "Moisten it, slave girl. Lubricate it well, warm it with your tongue … for your own sake."

A moment later, Martuska understood her Mistress's intention: the hook vanished from her mouth and pressed instead between her buttocks. Martuska felt her anus twitching as the metal kissed that most private, shameful part of her. She tightened instinctively, then did her best to relax as the curved metal pressed and twisted its way inside.

The friction broke. The slave girl's body yielded.

But Mistress Dominique didn't push the steel ball fully inside. Instead she held her slave girl there, balanced on the widest part of that spittle-slick sphere, so that she was held open, stretched and extended to the maximum possible extent. Martuska heard soft chuckling, so close to her ear that she could feel her Mistress's warm breath as the other woman twisted it again, moving it in and out, toying with her, owning her.

Then she slid it fully inside, permitting Martuska's straining ring of muscle to relax around the thinner metal of the hook. The slave girl felt her whole body sagging with relief.

But Mistress Dominique was not done with this game. She slowly withdrew the ball, just far enough to stretch Martuska fully open around its circumference again, and she held her there once more.

The slave girl realized that her Mistress had found a new way to own her, to possess the tight vulnerable ring of her ass. She couldn't keep herself from resisting — but resistance was impossible. She heard herself moan … from apprehension … from degradation … from desire.

Instantly, Mistress Dominique thrust the hook deep inside her … and left it there. It was as if she'd been waiting for her slave girl to signal her acceptance — enjoyment, even — of what was being done to her, before bringing the humiliation to an end.

The ball whose presence had been so all-consuming, vanished deep into Martuska's body where she was scarcely aware of it any more. She could still feel the cool, curved, alien weight nestled between her buttocks, though. She could still feel herself twitching around the smooth transfixing steel.

Mistress Dominique yanked Martuska's new ponytail down, hard. She heard the hook and the ring clicking together … so that the slightest movement of her head … the smallest attempt to hunch herself against the coming whipping … would press the hook even more painfully into the slave girl's core.

She felt the whipping frame creaking against her taut limbs. She felt renewed tension at her wrists and ankles as Mistress Dominique stretched her body further, cinched the hemp rope tighter. Martuska was now utterly open to her owner, available for whatever else she decided to do.

What she decided to do, apparently, was nothing.

Footsteps receded, and then Martuska's world became silent apart from her own breathing, and the thumping of her heart. She attempted to flex her body; the whipping post creaked again but didn't move. She twisted her head blindly, attempting to pinpoint the smallest sound that might betray someone's presence.

Silence. Not so much as a scuff of a high heel on stone, or the shuffling of a slave girl's bare feet, or the whisper of leather or silk.

Mistress Dominique, it seemed, was gone.

*

"Alex?"

"We'd better not talk," he said in a low voice. "But … you look beautiful like that." He cursed himself even as the words left his mouth; she didn't care if she looked beautiful, she cared about what was happening to her.

It was true, though. Martuska's body, arched and stretched out on that torture frame, was an exquisite sight.

"Are we alone?" she asked.

"Yes."

"I'm going to be okay," she told him. "It might not seem that way, but I will be."

Before he could say anything else, high-heeled footsteps sounded in the corridor outside. Mistress Dominique was returning.

*

Martuska felt the cool gloved hand on her back again. She couldn't see what her Mistress was doing. She couldn't tell if her tormentor was alone, or if the slave girl Lara had returned too.

Heel tips clicked as Mistress Dominique moved away. Martuska supposed that she'd gone to fetch a whip or a riding crop from one of the wall hooks — and yes, the chosen instrument swished through the air, cut against something with a fierce cracking sound. Martuska couldn't keep herself from sobbing, because the impact seemed more intense than anything Mistress Dominique had done to her before. Much more intense.

She'd spoken words of comfort to Alex, but she already knew it would be more than she could bear.

And so it was, when the first stroke bloomed on her buttocks. This wasn't like any of Mistress Dominique's previous punishments. Those had been in her bedroom — in a soft, warm, feminine space that lent itself more to playfulness than to torture.

This was her dungeon.

Another stroke blossomed and she threw herself against her bonds — except she couldn't move, she was trussed so tightly, transfixed so firmly, bent so submissively in her Mistress's punishment frame. The whip was inexorable. It struck again, and again, and again, and no matter what Martuska did, no matter how much she pleaded, she couldn't make it stop.

She couldn't escape. She couldn't do a single thing to save herself.

Her Mistress struck again and again, and she couldn't make it stop.

At last there came a pause.

"What would you sacrifice, in order to earn release?"

It took Martuska a moment to reclaim her lungs from sobbing, but she managed to reply, "Anything, Mistress ... I'll do anything you command, suffer whatever punishment you choose ... any other punishment ... as long as the whip goes away ... please take the whip away ... even if it's only for a while."

Mistress Dominique's only reply came from her whip, which returned with even more cruelty than before.

After a time, she asked, "What would you like to do for *me?*"

Martuska controlled her weeping for long enough to offer the only thing she possessed that might tempt Mistress Dominique to cease this punishment.

"I beg to be allowed to kneel and to worship you with my mouth."

"You do not deserve that honor," Mistress Dominique told her coldly. "You are in disgrace. A disgraced slave girl does not deserve such rewards. A disgraced slave girl only deserves to be bound, and hooked, and whipped."

For that moment, at least, Martuska knew that her Mistress's words were true.

Sight returned: the blindfold was gone.

Lara was standing before the whipping post — though it was hard for Martuska to see, because her plaited hair was still held captive by that relentless hook, yanking at the skin of her scalp and plunging the curved steel deeper into her body whenever she tried to tilt her head forward.

Mistress Dominique joined the red-headed slave girl; they stood face to face, Lara several inches shorter because of her owner's stiletto heels. The girl shrugged off her shift, revealing her flawless rump, her perfect breasts, the smooth juicy peach of her pussy. She knelt, pushing the curtain of fiery-colored hair clear of her face, clear of her mouth. Mistress threaded her fingers into those submissively lowered tresses and pulled the slave girl's lips to the dark curls between her own legs.

Martuska found herself straining at the hook, against her own ponytail, because she wanted to watch.

Mistress Dominique's first orgasm came quickly. Her second climax seemed more leisurely. Her third was even longer coming ... but the slave girl didn't tire until her Mistress was done with her. Martuska watched the girl as she worked, envying her naked beauty and her freedom, envying her even more when Mistress Dominique raised her up and whispered some intimacy into her ear.

They left hand-in-hand. Martuska knew that was done for show: to punish her. Mistress Dominique was not the kind of woman to link fingers with a slave girl, unless she had a good, pragmatic reason for doing so. Even so, in her present state of mind — helpless, still burning from the whip, grateful that her torment was over, aroused from what she'd just seen — Martuska couldn't help the pang of envy that ran through her.

Behind her, a solenoid buzzed and then jolted: the cell had unlocked itself. A moment later, she heard that door creaking open as Alex emerged from the space where he'd been imprisoned.

*

Alex's collar tingled, directing him to the dungeon's screen. He wanted to go straight to Martuska, but he was afraid that any defiance on his part would bring retribution on her; he wasn't about to risk making her situation even worse.

So he checked to see what he was expected to do.

Unchain Martuska and take her to the Spa. A treatment room has been unlocked for you. You may tend to her but you will avoid inappropriate activities.

He strode to the whipping post where he unclipped the chain that tethered the cruel, piercing hook to the girl's plaited hair. He asked her if he should remove the hook, but she seemed unable to speak so he left it in place. Instead, he unknotted the hemp rope, dismayed to see how angrily it had bitten into the slave girl's bare skin. Her delicate ankles came next, and he winced to see how her struggles had chafed them. He left her wrist bonds for last because he wasn't sure how well she'd be able to stand — and he judged rightly in that, because the girl collapsed against him as he unbuckled the final strap.

He lifted her as if she were his bride about to cross his threshold. Martuska's head rested on his shoulder with her long weighted ponytail bumping rhythmically against his side, as he carried her from the dungeon.

*

They encountered no one as Alex's collar led him through the mansion, to the wing that housed the Spa, and finally to the treatment area. The corridors had been chilly, but once inside the room, the temperature was comfortable for their naked bodies. The place was provided with a shower cubicle, bath robes, a massage table covered with toweling, a linen-closet, and several other cabinets that turned out to contain cooling lotions and sweetly-scented oils. A counter ran along one wall, stocked with instruments, gloves, wipes, and various receptacles.

He set Martuska on the table gently, face down. Then he touched the hook, so lightly that it barely moved under his finger. "Can I take this out?"

The girl nodded, so he began to ease the steel out as gently as he could. The first few inches came easily, but then the balled end must have encountered the constriction of her anus, because it refused to move any further.

"Twist it," she murmured. "Let it out slowly, with just enough pressure to keep it moving. You barely need to do any work at all."

Alex complied. Slowly but surely, the steel sphere began to appear. First it seemed like nothing more than a hint of brightness inside her, but then the smooth rounded surface began to appear. He watched in fascination as the slave girl's twitching ring of muscle expanded, enlarging itself to allow the passage of the ball. As it reached its maximum diameter, she told him, "Hold it there for a moment … I like how it feels."

He was tempted to slide it a little further out, and then back in, but Mistress Dominique might have viewed that as an 'inappropriate activity' so he just kept his hand still for a few seconds. Then he eased the sphere out completely. It looked perfectly clean as he set it down in a plastic tray.

He opened the first cabinet and studied the ranked jars of balms and unguents. "I wonder which of these will be best?" he wondered.

"The tall green bottle on the left," she said.

"You've been here before?" he asked in surprise.

"I've helped other slave girls … and boys," she said. "But I've never been whipped like that myself."

He took down the bottle and brought it to the massage table, but Martuska sat up painfully and put a hand on his arm. "I'd like to take a cool, soothing shower first," she said. "The temperature I need might feel a bit cold to you … but I'd like you to join me."

"Are you sure that won't cause more … trouble?" he asked.

"We mustn't touch one another intimately."

"So as long as I don't touch your pussy…"

"…and I don't touch your cock…"

"…then we should be okay?"

She nodded and they went into the cubicle together, where Martuska adjusted the flow as she desired. After a while she turned her back so that he could gently work soap suds into the burning flesh of her buttocks and thighs.

"That's nice," she said. "That helps."

Afterward he dried her with extreme care, and then he laid her back on the massage table and set to work with the healing oil.

Her rump and the backs of her thighs felt hot and feverish, deeply-flushed, crossed and recrossed by the marks of Mistress Dominique's riding crop. Alex would normally have warmed the lotion in his hands, but he decided to drizzle it on directly in the hope that the girl would benefit from its cooling effect. Martuska's sigh of relief told him he'd judged rightly. He worked as gently as he could, spreading the transparent stuff across her hot skin with featherlike fingertips. She sighed again. After a while, she asked him to move up to her back, and he spent several pleasurable minutes easing away tension from her spine and her shoulder blades.

"Now I'd like you to massage my buttocks again, and then work your way down my legs until you reach my feet," she said. "I'll let you know when to stop."

Alex hadn't realized how hard his cock was, until that moment. He almost had to bite his tongue to keep from saying, "Yes Mistress." He was glad he managed to stop himself. Saying such a thing might have been judged as inappropriate; Martuska was only a slave girl after all.

*

Four jolts: proceed directly to the dungeon.

It was the next morning and Alex had just finished breakfast. He'd been about to return to his room to check the screen there; the servants' hall had two of the devices, but they were always in use at this time of day. Now, he didn't need to bother.

He made his way along the corridor with its paintings and prints, pausing outside the door for long enough to strip. He glanced down. Still perfectly smooth. He wondered when his next treatment — the one that would begin to denude him permanently — would begin.

There was no time for such speculation. He was expected inside. Alex placed his hand on the door and entered the dungeon.

"Hello, slave boy. Come in and join us."

His cock stiffened in response to Mistress Dominique's greeting, then bounced fully into life as he saw Martuska. The slave girl stood against the far wall, tethered by two leather bracelets that matched her collar, so that her arms were loosely extended to either side. Apart from those bonds she was naked.

Mistress Dominique waited near the whipping post, resting her left hand on one of the slanting timbers. In her right hand she held a long riding crop. A small table stood just behind her, upon which sat an ornate box.

And lounging in the dungeon's wing-backed chair with her leather-clad, spike-heeled legs stretched out in front of her, was the voluptuous, cat-suited form of Madam Fen.

Mistress Dominique swished her riding crop through the air, then extended it toward Alex. "I treated myself to a gift a few days ago," she told him. "Isn't it just perfect?"

He nodded. "Yes, Mistress."

"Come here and look at it."

Alex felt his heart beating faster as he approached. His Mistress's personal magnetism was almost enough to make him forget the presence of Martuska, beautiful and naked in her chains. Almost, but not quite.

"Take *your* end in your hand," she commanded. "Grip it firmly, so you can feel how it responds as I move *my* end."

Obediently, he took hold of the whip where it narrowed toward the leather tongue. It was long, flexible, made of fine braided leather over a strong supple core. Mistress Dominique shifted and twisted the handle, letting him sense how whippy it was and how cruel it would be.

"An ideal instrument," she said, "for correcting a naughty slave. Perfect for a light whipping … or for a thorough chastisement such as I administered yesterday. Didn't I, Martuska?"

"Yes, Mistress."

"If only you could have been here, Madam Fen."

"I would surely have appreciated it," Madam Fen said. Alex felt distinctly uneasy about the open hostility with which the woman regarded Martuska's chained form. Her next words did nothing to alleviate his concern: "I would have enjoyed witnessing such a thing. A slave who takes the property of a Mistress should be corrected *most* severely."

Mistress Dominique arched one perfect eyebrow. "I thought your preference was to … indulge the masochistic needs of *male* slaves?"

"Sometimes one comes across a female who is even more deserving," Madam Fen said. She rose to approach Martuska, placing her fingertips on the girl's outstretched arm, just inside her elbow, then stroking that captive flesh until she reached the leather bracelet that encircled the slave girl's delicate wrist. "Perhaps there will be another opportunity."

"If so, then I shall inform you." Mistress Dominique's tone was placating. "Or I can arrange for either of these slaves to spend the night in your suite, if you wish."

Madam Fen moved back into the center of the room. "You already know what really interests me, Dominique."

"Of course. You enjoy personal ownership more than guest-privileges. I understand that."

"Yet in this case…"

"I have other stock available for purchase," Mistress Dominique continued smoothly. "I anticipate the imminent arrival of several remarkable specimens."

But Madam Fen's attention was entirely absorbed by Martuska's naked body. "Once I have set my mind on possessing something," she murmured, "then that is the thing I must possess."

"Your interest is understandable … and appreciated. I deeply regret that the item you desire is unavailable."

Alex's head was spinning as he struggled to understand what was going on. Madam Fen must have offered to buy Martuska, he thought. That was a dismaying possibility. The woman was wantonly cruel, for one thing. And even if she'd been the kindest Mistress imaginable, it would still mean that Martuska would vanish from the mansion, and from Alex's life.

Fortunately, Mistress Dominique had clearly not agreed to the sale. He remembered that first breakfast in the servants' hall, when Lara had hinted that females were exempt from being transferred to new owners. How had she put it? Something about only ever having heard of boys being sold. If that were true, Martuska would be safe and Alex had nothing to worry about.

But Lara hadn't said that girls were *never* sold, and Alex had an inkling of how wealthy, how powerful, Madam Fen was. She certainly seemed to be accustomed to getting her own way.

"We clearly have much to discuss," Mistress Dominique said. "But for now, shall we accommodate our immediate desires?"

Madam Fen's malevolent attention had still been focused on Martuska but now she turned toward Alex. "Of course," she said. "Please begin whenever you are ready."

"Thank you, Madam Fen." Mistress Dominique gestured toward Alex by flicking the long whip through the air; he cringed at the swishing sound, imagined how the whip's bite would feel on his naked skin. "Get to your knees, slave boy. I want to see how you respond to my … riding crop. Or should I say *your* riding crop, because I mean to reserve it for you. The only other person who has felt it, is Martuska. You saw me use it on her, didn't you?"

Alex nodded. "Yes, Mistress."

"You are to be its next subject," she told him. "You and Martuska alone shall feel its sting. Each of you will come to know the instrument intimately, as the three of us explore it together." She and glanced at Madam Fen, "Or perhaps it will be the four of us. Neither of its subjects will ever forget that it has only ever been used on one other slave. And should one subject be sold, the riding crop shall be included in the price."

He felt the beginnings of panic. *Should one subject be sold.* Perhaps Martuska wasn't safe after all. The fact that Madam Fen — who was gazing hungrily at the chained slave girl again — might wish to be included in this perverted foursome, was terrifying. Why would she be interested?

He knew why. He knew all to well.

With his mind's eye he saw Jasper again. He recalled how the unfortunate slave boy had been purchased and enjoyed by Madam Fen, and then sent out the next day to trudge around the yard, his head hooded and hidden and his naked body whipped raw.

Was that in store for Martuska?

Alex knew he'd never be able to accept that.

"Look at me!"

His attention snapped back to Mistress Dominique.

"Stand up, slave boy. Thighs well apart." Once he'd obeyed, she reached down between his legs. She had no gloves on today; her fingers felt cool — and stronger than their slender elegance implied — as she claimed his cock.

Immediately, he was fully aroused. He couldn't remember when he'd last been allowed to come. He couldn't have stopped himself from responding to this desirable, dominant woman, even if he'd wanted to. Even Madam Fen's terrifying touch would have been irresistible to him.

"Good," Mistress Dominique said. "You're nice and smooth … and nice and hard, too."

He felt her hand moving downward, and then her fingertips were gently exploring the naked skin of his scrotum. She glanced at Madam Fen. "Like velvet," she said.

"The skill and dedication of your beautician is admirable," the other woman said. "She would be in great demand at my home in Shanghai."

Mistress Dominique laughed. "That one is certainly not for sale, but you are welcome to bring someone here to be trained, if you like." She turned back to Alex. "How does it feel to be so vulnerable? How does it feel when I squeeze your balls like this?"

The sudden pressure made him gasp.

"It hurts, doesn't it?"

"Yes, Mistress."

"Good."

Martuska's chains jangled as she shifted position.

"Look at my tethered beauty over there, slave boy," Mistress Dominique said. "Appreciate her grace, her nakedness. What do you like best about her in that pose?"

Alex gazed at the girl. "I like everything about her, Mistress."

"Do you like … how her arms are captured by my shackles, so they're stretched out to either side?"

There could be no denying it: he did. "Yes, Mistress."

"Do you like how her back is arched? She doesn't need to stand like that, you know. She's doing it to make a pleasing composition … do you think she might be doing that for you, perhaps?"

Alex swallowed. "I hope so, Mistress."

Mistress Dominique smiled. "How about her breasts? Are they firm enough for you? A little small, perhaps? Do you like how pertly she presents those rosy nipples?"

"I think they're perfect, Mistress."

"Let's see if we can improve things even more. Slave girl! Bring your knees closer together … now bend them to the left a little, so that your whole body makes a single sweet curve. Now relax your arms, so they drape naturally from the chains."

Martuska obeyed.

"I can feel from your cock that you like her even more now," Mistress Dominique said. *"I certainly like her even more. How about you, Madam Fen?"*

"Her limbs make a pleasing composition."

"Well, slave boy, do you agree with my colleague?" Mistress Dominique asked — and before Alex could even draw a breath to reply, she snapped, "Don't answer that!"

Crack!

The riding crop cut lightly across his naked flank.

"From now on, you're not to say a single word until I give you permission. Madam Fen and I *might* find uses for your mouth … your tongue … but they will not involve speech."

She reached into the box on the table, and produced a small device.

"Look at this, slave boy. Do you know what it is?"

Alex nodded. He'd seen a chastity cage before, though the one Miranda had used on him had been equipped with a padlock. This one seemed to be higher-tech and had no obvious release mechanism.

It looked quite a bit smaller, too.

"It has a fingerprint sensor instead of a key," Mistress Dominique told him. "It can be released only by *my* touch." She set the device back down. "Stand with your back to the whipping frame. Try to arrange yourself attractively." She waited as Alex complied, and then pursed her lips disapprovingly. "You have such a lot to learn … and I have so little time … so many slaves to train. Perhaps I will permit my beautiful, graceful Martuska to teach you. You'd better keep your hands off her, this time."

Crack!

"Put your arms up against the posts."

He hated to obey, to offer himself like a sacrificial victim, but what choice was there?

Mistress Dominique secured his wrists. "Now. Arch your back … open yourself … display yourself. There's no need for me to bind your ankles, as long as you submit. That's better. Your cock belongs to *me*. In a little while, I shall claim it."

She was partly behind him now, but he heard her opening the box again. A moment later and her hand was on his cock again … cold and slippery from some kind of oil. She rubbed him, up and down, up and down, too lightly to offer him anything except the ghost of what he really needed. He suppressed a groan.

"That feels good, doesn't it?" she crooned. "Or do you need me to squeeze a little harder? Hmmm. I don't think so. This feels good to *me* … and that's the only thing that counts."

Alex glanced at Madam Fen. To his consternation, she seemed oblivious to the show that Mistress Dominique was putting on … not that he wanted the cruel woman's attention, but it would have been better on him than on Martuska … and it was to the chained slave girl that the woman's cat-like eyes were directed.

"How hard you are," Mistress Dominique murmured. "I'm pleased that my property is so masculine. So virile. So well proportioned. I think you might even make a satisfactory lover, if I ever decided to sample you like that."

The thought that any woman might allow him into her pussy again made his body spasm, and Mistress Dominique chuckled. "You want that, don't you? You want to fuck me, don't you, slave boy?"

Alex wasn't sure whether she expected him to deny it, or acknowledge it.

"Don't look so worried. You're allowed to *want* to fuck me. You're just not allowed to actually do it."

She kept working her hand up and down. Much too gently, but at least she hadn't stopped.

"Or perhaps you're hoping that I'll unchain my slave girl, and order her to pleasure you orally? To accept your hard cock into her warm, wet, willing mouth. To bob her pretty head back … and forward … in … and out…"

She moved her hand in time with her words, as if to pantomime what she described.

"…until you shoot your load into her mouth? Until your spunk is oozing between her lips?"

He glanced at Martuska. She hadn't moved from her commanded pose, not even by an inch. Her face betrayed nothing.

"Perhaps you're even hoping that I'll order her to swallow. That would be nice, wouldn't it? You're allowed to want it … but …"

Mistress Dominique shook her head and made a tutting noise.

"No."

She continued to work him. "Maybe I'll keep going like this until you can't bear it any more. Until your only desire is that I will permit you to come … in my oiled hands." She sighed. "But that's not allowed, either."

Still she caressed him with her slick fingers, light as feathers.

"Perhaps you'd settle for the boon of my oiled, bare feet. To be permitted to rub yourself between my naked soles until…"

She sighed again. "But no. That would be much too messy. Your cum would splash all over my feet. It might even dribble between my toes. I suppose I might enjoy forcing you to lick up every drop of the mess you'd made … but … no. That's not what I have in mind for you. Not today."

She gave a final squeeze, a little harder than the others, so that Alex couldn't keep himself from moaning.

"And now … my caresses stop."

Her hand was gone from him.

"Poor slave boy. Did you think I'd keep going? When I said I would claim your cock … did you think I meant it for your pleasure?"

She picked up the chastity device again.

"No. I am going to claim my slave boy with steel."

She showed him a gleaming ring, cunningly hinged. "This will trap *everything…*"

Almost before he knew it, the slender shackle had encircled his genitals. He couldn't help shivering at the metal's chilly, entrapping touch. Blood was pumping into his cock, engorging the flesh so that it swelled uselessly against the closing steel.

"How does that feel?" she breathed in his ear. "How does it feel to have your cock … and your balls … captured like that?" She squeezed and Alex felt the decisive click, even more than he heard it.

"Your manhood … is mine," Mistress Dominique told him. "Now for the tube."

She placed the cage's opening against the tip of his penis. It slid in easily at first, because of the oil with which she'd slicked him. But his cock was fully erect and straining toward release, not imprisonment.

"You don't want to be caged, do you?" she asked. "You're trying to resist. You want to fuck something, don't you?" She pressed harder but the tube would go no further. "I know what you want to fuck. Martuska. Go on, look at her. Don't try to deny it. You want to pump your cock in her sweet pussy, don't you? Yes, I think you want to fuck my slave girl."

Crack!

She flicked him with her riding crop again.

"That's not allowed. Pussies are not allowed. Not any more. The only thing you can fuck is this tight steel tube … but, poor slave boy, it's too small. Your hard prick won't fit." She twisted the cage, working it fractionally further on to his straining penis. "It feels good to try, doesn't it? Enjoy that pleasure while you can, slave boy."

Mistress Dominique withdrew the tube, then re-fitted as much of it as she could. "At least the head of your cock fits. Almost. There. The first inch … is inside."

She applied more oil, twisted and pushed again.

"Perhaps you should say goodbye to it. Perhaps your poor slave cock should make the most of this because pushing its way into my lubed cage is the most fun it's going to have, for a very long time."

Alex heard himself whimpering ... from the knowledge of what was being done to him, from the desire to be free and from the desire to be caged.

"*I* will decide when you earn your release. If you earn your release. I wouldn't hold my breath, if I were you."

As much as she tried, she couldn't get the cage to go any further. "If you don't submit to being caged," she told him, "I shall whip you. Severely."

Unfortunately, Alex was now in a mental place where that threat, delivered by that woman, aroused him even more...

Mistress Dominique shook her head. "You little slave slut. You're *hoping* for punishment, aren't you? You think you'll enjoy the whip."

She cut the riding crop through the air.

"Not the way I wield it. Look at Martuska. She knows. She doesn't want to feel it again. Not so soon at any rate, but she will, unless you obey me."

Alex realized he was faced with a choice: lose his erection so that Mistress Dominique could slide her cage onto his cock, or see Martuska suffer again. He didn't think he could bear that. He didn't think she could, either. So he closed his eyes and imagined himself elsewhere.

He was in the slave quarters, scrubbing out the ancient enamel bath. No matter what he did it would never sparkle, the surface was too old, too pitted, too stained. Then he had to clean the tiled floor. The string mop was old, its musty smell rising up as he worked...

"That's better," Mistress Dominique said as she slid and squeezed the cage until it had enclosed him completely. "That's right. Relax. Don't think about what I'm doing to you. Don't think about how helpless you're going to be from now on."

That wasn't helping. The more she described Alex's situation, the more his body wanted to get hard. Desperately he sought the slave's bathroom again, pictured every inch of that cracked and stained tile floor.

"Now, your world changes." She breathed the words so quietly he could barely hear them. On the other hand, the metallic click with which she emphasized her point was perfectly audible.

The sound and the steely sensation made his cock surge back into life ... except it couldn't. Not fully. Hardly at all, in fact.

"Poor slave boy is allowed to *try* to get hard," she told him, in tones of pretended sympathy. "I don't mind that. You'll be able to get a *little* hard, inside my cage. You'll have just enough space to keep you permanently aroused and eager to please." She brought her right palm up to his face, extending all five digits to show him the fingerprint whorls at their ends. "These are the only things that can release you."

Madam Fen had seated herself again and now she stretched in her chair. "I've had one or two possessions try to escape by other means," she said. "After a few months of confinement they can become inventively determined to be free."

Mistress Dominique nodded. "But this slave boy doesn't want Martuska to suffer." She stared at him. "Do you, slave boy?"

Alex shook his head.

"If I even suspect that you are trying to free yourself, to cheat in any way, then I will make your beautiful friend wish she'd never been born. Do you understand?"

Alex nodded. He knew that he'd never try to release himself, if it meant putting Martuska at risk.

Mistress Dominique unbuckled his wrists. "Turn around," she ordered him, and moments later he found himself restrained again, this time with his back facing away from the whipping post.

He wondered if there would be a blindfold and a rope and a hook for him, as there had been for Martuska.

"Come over here, slave girl," Mistress Dominique commanded, and Alex saw that Martuska hadn't really been shackled to the wall: her wrist bonds were merely hooked onto their chains so she was able to release herself. She did so, and approached the punishment frame.

"Can you reach the cage?" Mistress Dominique asked her.

Martuska stooped and put her hand between two timbers, just below the point where they crossed. Alex sensed her fingers brushing the metal that encased him.

"I can, Mistress."

"Good. Then you shall fondle him, to whatever extent that's possible now, while I whip him. We will begin with a dozen hard strokes."

Martuska gripped the cage and began to move her fist up and down along its length. Though Alex could barely feel it, the fleeting sensation of her fingertips was still enough to drive him wild. From somewhere close behind him, he heard Mistress Dominique's riding crop cutting the air. His body jerked at the stinging impact, and Martuska lost her grip on him. He tried to hold still for her as the second blow fell…

"How gentle you are," Madam Fen observed dryly.

The third stroke seemed crueler, but Alex couldn't tell if it was because of the cat-suited woman's taunt, or because his skin was becoming sensitized.

Martuska was pressing harder, too, as if she wanted to get through the steel barrier that separated his cock from her hand. But no matter how much she squeezed, all Alex could feel was the gentlest of touches, in those few places where his flesh bulged between the bars.

He wondered whether the whipping would become so severe that he'd lose his erection altogether. If that happened, his penis would shrivel inside its steel prison and the comforting contact of Martuska's fingers would recede even further. He looked down at the slave girl, crouched in front of him as she reached up between the timber beams. Her hand moved back and forward; the riding crop struck again.

He was still hard. As long as he kept looking at Martuska, he knew he'd stay hard.

Another stroke, and another. He'd lost count now. Could he really endure twelve? Would there be more than twelve?

We shall begin with a dozen hard strokes.

Alex remembered the torment that Martuska had endured. It didn't seem possible that he would escape more lightly.

Another stroke, and another, and he was still hard, still fascinated by the kneeling slave girl.

"There," Mistress Dominique said. "We can move on to the main entertainment. Would you care to blindfold him, Madam Fen?"

"With pleasure."

"Then we shall have Martuska whip him while we watch. Slave girl, you are to chastise him thoroughly. If I think you're holding back, I'll put you in his place. Do I make myself clear?"

"Yes Mistress."

Alex sensed Madam Fen approaching from behind, and then she dropped a thick black bag over his head. He felt her tightening and securing the drawstring about his neck.

Now he was in darkness. He strained to hear what was happening, but his world had fallen silent. Martuska was naked and barefoot and so naturally noiseless in the dungeon, but the others both wore clicking stilettos. Still, Alex could hear neither of them. He waited. Nothing happened and he wondered if all three women had crept away to leave him alone, as Mistress Dominique and Lara had done during Martuska's punishment.

Then he heard the crop cutting through the air again.

Thwack!

"One," Martuska said. Then she kept striking. And counting.

"Two."

"Three."

His rump felt as if it were on fire. He steeled himself not to cry out or to struggle. After a while he couldn't keep himself from gasping in pain as each new blow fell, re-igniting flesh already smoldering from previous insults. He began to twist his body against the whipping post, too, though he knew that was hopeless. Mistress Dominique had strapped him in too securely for his efforts to make the slightest bit of difference.

"Twenty three."

"Twenty four."

There was a pause, and he felt Martuska's body brushing against his own. "Have you had enough?" she whispered close to his ear. Her arm snaked between the oak post and his torso; her fingers found his penis cage again.

His body responded to her. His cock pressed at its bars like a caged animal, starved for its owner's feather-like touch.

Inside the darkness of his enclosing hood, Alex began to nod, then restrained himself. If she let him off too lightly, she'd be punished herself.

"Do what you need to do," he muttered. Someone tugged on the strings of the black bag that had robbed him of sight, then removed it. After that perfect darkness even the candlelit dungeon seemed suddenly too bright. While his eyes adjusted, he twisted his head to look for Mistress Dominique and Madam Fen, but saw neither of them. Martuska released his ankle bonds, then his wrists. He staggered back from the whipping post and she braced him with one slim shoulder. Now he could turn fully around.

Apart from the two of them, the dungeon was empty.

"Where—?"

"They left before I'd even begun."

"But I didn't hear anything."

"They took their shoes off," Martuska said. "They like messing with our heads."

"So … they wouldn't have known, if you hadn't whipped me?"

Martuska smiled at him. "Like I said, I did what I needed to do. Now, shall we find our way back to that massage room in the Spa?"

*

In the following weeks and months, Alex was kept busy.

His days were spent turning the mill machinery to provide flour for the mansion's kitchen, or cutting and splitting firewood for its many hearths, or tending to the hedges and dry stone walls that kept the livestock in their enclosures and away from the estate's cropland. He'd never been much for the outdoors, but he took to it readily enough: learning new skills was enjoyable.

The regime of physical labor made his body leaner and harder than he'd have imagined possible at the urban gym he'd once used.

Most evenings he had to himself. Whenever Martuska was free too, she'd come to his room so they could sit and talk. Restraining themselves from any activities that might get them into trouble was a continual struggle. Even locked into the chastity cage, there were things Alex would have liked to do with her, and for her.

On other nights, the bell would summon him to his screen, which would send him to a guest bedroom. There, he'd spend hours pleasuring whichever of Mistress Dominique's friends had taken enough of a liking to him during the day to desire his night-time attendance.

Some of the women wanted a bath attendant, as Miranda had done on that first memorable evening. Others wished for a whipping boy, or to be serviced orally. A handful were into strap-on sex. Alex hated that, but the more he strained against the invasion, the hornier the women got. In the end, he learned that it was better not to resist. Even so, he'd feel sore for days after a dildo enthusiast was done with him.

Madam Fen summoned him one night and required all of the above.

His most memorable assignation was with a 'Mistress Patricia', whose fingerprints had been authorized to remove his chastity device. As the woman pressed the sensor that would unlock him, she mentioned the price she'd paid for this privilege. It was an eye-watering sum, but then Alex had come to understand that these elite females had an unusual attitude to money. They dealt in a more privileged coinage: favors, handshakes, private pleasures.

Mistress Patricia had pulled his cage off, allowing his cock to spring to life. It had been weeks since Alex was last freed. She'd ordered him to fuck her immediately; he'd exploded almost before he was inside her. The woman seemed to have been half-expecting that, but she still took the opportunity to correct her slave's 'shortcoming' with a thick leather strap. She didn't strike nearly as hard as Madam Fen would have. As soon as Alex was ready, Mistress Patricia had enjoyed him again, and continued to do so, in various ways, until the sky lightened outside the windows of her suite.

The guests who summoned him to their beds were of every type: slender and stout; tall and short; blonde and brunette; busty and petite. Yet once he found himself in their varied presences, he seemed to lose all inhibitions.

Their feminine attraction was irresistible, and that inflamed his submissive desire to serve and please them. The only thing he could imagine that might have defeated these urges would have been Martuska's expressed desire that he cease.

And that was exceedingly strange, he thought; Martuska was only a slave girl, while the women who used him were fully-fledged Mistresses.

Through rumor and deduction, he gradually pieced together a better picture of the mansion, its owner, and the merchant bank she ran.

The week-long parties were an important part of the bank's business. Invitations were highly prized. Mistress Dominique's senior clients were always welcome but others had to wait their turn. Some of these occasional guests were powerful businesswomen who'd been sounded out and were now being offered a glimpse of the fringe-benefits the bank could offer; some were employees like Miranda, going about the work of procuring and delivering slaves; others were simply like-minded females who'd been fortunate enough to catch Mistress Dominique's eye.

Madam Fen, he observed, seldom missed the opportunity to join in the fun.

He remained locked in his chastity cage almost permanently. During the first few months he'd be released when attending the Spa for his depilation appointments, because the beautician needed to access every inch of him. Then, once she'd declared him to be permanently denuded of body hair (which would have dismayed him, if Martuska hadn't already mentioned that she preferred him that way), even those brief periods of respite came to an end. From then on, apart from that one memorable night with Mistress Patricia, his only opportunities for release came while chained to Mistress Dominique's whipping post.

It would be done this way: first, he would attend Mistress Dominique in the inner chambers of her dungeon. These reminded Alex of the guest suite where he'd thought he was going to stay with Miranda: a luxurious bathroom; a sitting room; a small study with a desk-mounted interface screen; a well-appointed bedroom suitable for a Mistress to receive oral worship — or whatever other services she required — from her slave. Martuska would often be present, but she would wait outside, in the dungeon itself.

Mistress Dominique might appear pleased by Alex's tongue, but over weeks and months of servitude he became convinced that she never seemed entirely sated. Alex felt there was a fire in her that burned brighter with each commanded climax and — regardless of the tireless efforts he expended — was never fully extinguished. When they left her bed behind and re-entered the dungeon, her skin would be hot as if with a fever, and her eyes would be bright.

Martuska knew what was expected; she'd be waiting by the punishment frame. Alex would watch as his Mistress administered a light whipping — nothing too severe, because slave girls were not subjected to harsh discipline unless they'd been seriously disobedient — but it was still enough to make Martuska gasp as the crop repeatedly stung her naked flesh.

Nothing had been as cruel as the slave girl's punishment after their bathroom encounter. For Martuska's sake, Alex was glad that the locked chastity cage prevented any repeat of *that* particular infraction.

Not that either of them would have dared.

Mistress Dominique would often be so turned-on by this point, that she'd order one of them to orally service her again — usually in the dungeon itself; occasionally back in her chamber. Once the slaves had performed these pleasurable duties, Alex would take his place at the punishment frame. Martuska would kneel in front of him, as she had on the first occasion he'd been whipped. Mistress Dominique would stand behind him, wielding her riding crop more forcefully now.

Her target was male, after all.

She would command Alex to remain perfectly still, no matter how much pain she inflicted.

If he managed to satisfy her in that, she might consider reaching around to press her finger against the sensor panel that would free his penis. She would then resume his whipping as Martuska used her oiled hand to bring him as close as possible to ejaculation … and she was commanded to do this with clinical efficiency, with a view to milking him, not massaging him.

Once Alex was trembling at the brink, Mistress Dominique would either nod to grant his climax … or shake her head to deny it. If she nodded, Martuska would murmur "Come," and continue for another stroke or two until he ejaculated. He'd be relieved, but also full of regret that his pleasure was over almost before it had begun.

All too often, Mistress Dominique would decide that he was to remain frustrated. Then, Alex felt nothing but despair.

Either way, he'd be locked up again immediately.

At least the slave girl's hand was something, he thought. At least it was Martuska.

*

Occasionally, he wondered about what was happening in the world he'd left behind. Had Miranda been offered the junior partnership she wanted? Had she found another submissive man to seduce and enslave? Would Alex see her some day, arriving with her latest offering, at one of the big house parties?

Even if he did, so what? Miranda now seemed like someone he knew long ago, in a different life. As long as she left him alone, he'd be fine. There was no need to feel bad about her.

Alex did feel a little bad about the local firms he'd once helped with their computer needs. He'd enjoyed the work, even if it paid a pittance compared to what he might have earned in a more corporate setting. Those small business owners had relied on him and he'd just disappeared.

He missed messing around with computers, too. He'd been quite the hacker, back in the day. He remembered Miranda using that as her excuse, when she turned down his suggestion of working at the bank. That hadn't been her real reason, of course. The real reason was that he was the wrong gender, but that didn't mean Miranda's first assessment had been wrong.

Most of all he worried about Madam Fen. He couldn't help noticing how the cat-suited woman stared at Martuska whenever she stayed at the mansion. He still didn't think Mistress Dominique wanted to sell the slave girl, but he'd asked around among the other slaves, and the consensus was that if Madam Fen wanted something badly enough, she'd spend whatever it took to get it.

The only question for Alex was, did Martuska fall into that prized category? Would Madam Fen offer a sum that Mistress Dominique wouldn't be able to refuse? The price might not even be paid in cash, he thought. Madam Fen had political influence too. She could smooth the way, provide introductions and recommendations, make life easier for a merchant bank seeking to expand in the Far East.

He clung to the fact that Madam Fen liked boys, a fact that he knew from personal experience. That knowledge sustained him in his hope that whatever Madam Fen saw in Martuska, was no more than a Mistress's idle fancy. It wasn't serious, he told himself; it would pass.

But what if it did not?

Alex decided that he had to find out before Madam Fen had a chance to swoop — and he worried that she might do that at the next house party, which was only a few days away. If his fears were well-founded then he would have no option but to warn Martuska and then to do his best to escape from the estate with her, if she agreed to such a scheme.

The only problem was that he was a slave in a mansion where slaves had no role except to serve and to obey. Uncovering forbidden information, and then executing a plan of his own, would require a distinctly un-slave-like level of resourcefulness, empowerment, responsibility … and defiance.

For Martuska's sake, he had to find a way to achieve those things.

*

On the eve of the week-long gathering, an idea finally came. A handful of guests had arrived early and one of these — a young female whom Alex hadn't seen before — had apparently decided to explore the mansion, including the shabbier parts that were usually reserved for the slaves. She was strolling along a corridor near the servants' hall, when Alex spied her.

A guest who was bored enough to explore the dingy slave quarters, might also be bored enough to amuse herself with a random slave for the next few hours. Alex had often been summoned to some bedroom or other, as he went about his business in the corridors; he was supposed to keep himself permanently available to serve the guests in any way they pleased. But today the clock was ticking. He needed time to think, to come up with a plan. So, he hung back.

The guest paused at the end of the corridor, near one of the wall-mounted screens. This unit was used almost exclusively by slaves picking up their orders, but it recognized other tracker implants, too. She waited, tapping her foot, while it brought up her personal menu with all the extra options available to her as a privileged guest. She opened a plan of the mansion and spent some moments poring over it, then set off with renewed confidence.

Once she'd moved on, Alex approached the screen. He knew exactly how close he'd be able to get before it picked up his own tracker. He paused, then pushed his left hand over that invisible boundary. The screen went blank instantly, and then (after the usual delay) it brought up his personal menu screen.

What secrets, thought Alex, might I discover if the thing wasn't able to detect my tracker?

As soon as the coast was clear, he made his way up to his room.

*

It was a strange sensation, seeking to enter Mistress Dominique's subterranean domain without first being summoned. Any sensible person would have avoided that place of pain and degradation altogether. Even a natural slave like Alex, locked in chastity and with no possibility of release except in that torture chamber, always felt a frisson of fear as he crossed the threshold.

Now he was here voluntarily but the trepidation was still there. It seemed to seep into him from the darkness, from the very stones.

The familiar submissive arousal was growing, too. Alex might be praying that the area was unoccupied, but his body knew nothing of such hopes. His caged cock had been trained to respond to this dungeon as a place of pleasure as well as of torment. Just being here made his penis stir in its too-small prison, and then strain against the steel bars.

He was breaking so many rules. He'd stolen the candle he used to light his way. He was fully clothed while entering a space were slaves were commanded to be naked. He was about as far from his room as it was possible to be, yet his neck was bare, his collar resting on its charging stand. And he'd wrapped his left hand in a thick, crude mitten made from the foil wrappings that Martuska had provided, when she'd given him the leftovers from that stolen picnic on their first day together.

Foil was made of aluminum. Aluminum blocked radio signals. That meant the mansion's tracking systems couldn't detect the microchip implanted at the base of his thumb. He'd approached several screens on the way down here; not one had responded. He was a ghost.

That was against the rules, too.

If Alex's plan worked, then he'd show up as being asleep in his chamber. Which was just where he ought to be, at this time of night…

He tilted his head, listening intently at the dungeon door. No sound came from within, no creaking of ropes or swishing of whips. No groaning or whimpering. No pleadings for mercy or cries of pain, no tap-tapping of stiletto heels on echoing stone.

Gently, he pushed the outer door open.

The main chamber was vacant. The panel that covered the confinement cell's window grating was in place so that even if someone were locked inside they wouldn't be able to see him — and even if they saw him, what could they do?

The true danger was that Mistress Dominique might now be in her suite of rooms adjoining the dungeon — exactly where Alex needed to be.

He crossed the floor and entered the passage that led to Mistress Dominique's suite. The only sounds were his footsteps and his breathing — the entire place appeared abandoned. The study was dark, the screen glowing with the last menu that Mistress Dominique had used. Alex sat at her desk, set down his candle-holder, and brought his chipped left hand nearer to the screen.

The display didn't change.

Mistress Dominique's privilege level showed as nine. Her account offered more options than Alex, with his lowly male-slave privilege of zero, had ever seen before.

He tapped on 'Messages' and began to hunt for anything mentioning property transfers, particularly relating to green-eyed slave girls of Hungarian extraction. The search function was complex but he'd used similar things before.

Here. He paused at a message mentioning the planned transfer of one of the mansion's slaves to a registrant referred to as 'M.F.' Alex could think of only one slave owner who had those initials:

Madam Fen.

If that cruel cat-woman was the purchaser, who could her prize be if not the slave girl that had absorbed so much of her attention recently?

Certainty had been a long time coming, but Alex finally knew that he had to get Martuska away from the mansion. He had to get himself away, too.

He continued exploring the rest of the system. Where was the option to signal slaves in their rooms? Martuska should be asleep at this time of night. He needed to bring her here. She'd have her collar on, so he had to find out how to release it, and since he didn't want to spend the rest of his life with his penis bound in steel he'd need to access the fingerprint database and reprogram his chastity cage.

Maybe he could add Martuska's prints to the system. His cock stiffened inside its steel prison as he imagined her releasing him. Or deciding not to.

But he couldn't afford to let his mind run away with pleasant fantasies. At some point, they'd need a car. Would the system tell him where the keys were kept? Was it possible to open the parking garage remotely? How about the main gates?

Within minutes, his investigations had so absorbed him that he was completely oblivious to the slow, careful opening of the door.

*

"Well, well, well."

Alex came back to reality with a jolt. Mistress Dominique was at the room's threshold, frowning at him. Behind her, he could see Madam Fen, dressed as always in her cat suit. A little further back, partly hidden in the shadowy passage that led from the dungeon, was a third leather-clad, masked Dominatrix.

"I always hoped you'd be a risk-taker," Mistress Dominique said.

He set his shoulders and glared at her. "I was stopping you from selling Martuska." He paused, then added, "Mistress."

"Sell *Martuska?*" Mistress Dominique began to laugh, then controlled herself. "How did you get *that* idea?" Before he could reply she continued, "Madam Fen likes boys. She wanted to buy you. I refused."

"Perhaps," the cat-woman said, "this act of defiance will make you reconsider."

"Perhaps," Mistress Dominique said. "Why don't we put our heads together to decide his fate?"

Madam Fen turned to gaze at the third woman lingering in the passageway. "I refuse to deal with a slave girl guilty of claiming the property of her betters." she snapped.

"She isn't a slave girl any more, but if you prefer not to involve her, I'll make the decision on my own."

"I warn you, if you just decide to give him to her anyway, I shall—"

"Don't worry," Mistress Dominique said. "You shall have your opportunity to win the prize you desire."

"How?"

At a signal from Mistress Dominique the third masked woman entered the room. She was dressed in supple black leather and smooth dark silk: corset, short skirt, stockings, and patent stiletto shoes which proved to be no obstacle to her lithe grace. Something about the way she moved…

"Martuska!" Alex called out her name before he could stop himself.

"Not quite," Mistress Dominique said dryly. "This is *Mistress* Martuska Farkas. Females choose to serve in my mansion solely so that they can learn to command. Didn't Mistress Miranda ever mention that she traveled the same path, not so long ago?"

Alex shook his head.

"Oh well, I suppose she must keep some things secret from her recruits." Mistress Dominique glanced at the other two women. "As the owner of this slave, I have decided to award him to the winner of a small test of skill. Who will take the first turn?"

"What are the rules?" Madam Fen demanded.

"I shall strip the slave naked, remove his chastity device, and arrange him so that he's available."

Madam Fen nodded. "And then?"

Mistress Dominique opened a drawer in her desk and produced a stopwatch. "Each of you will compel an orgasm from him, as quickly as you can. The faster performance wins, timed from first touch to the beginning of ejaculation."

"For how long has this slave been kept locked in chastity?"

Mistress Dominique shrugged. "I don't really keep track. A couple of weeks, at least. He's ready."

"Then whichever of us goes first will have a distinct advantage. This appears to be no contest at all."

"I've considered that," Mistress Dominique said. "Whoever takes the second turn may choose to use whatever perfume she wishes. This advantage will not be permitted to the first competitor."

"And you will be judge and time keeper?"

Mistress Dominique nodded.

"As one of your senior clients," Madam Fen said, "I expect to choose whether to go first or second."

"Agreed."

"Then I wish to go first."

Alex's heart sank. Madam Fen was no fool; she understood perfectly well that the weeks he'd spent locked into his steel cock cage had left his balls aching for release, full of pent-up energy that would be there for the first competitor to milk. As for the second competitor having access to 'perfume', well, he wasn't even sure what that meant. Miranda had often misted herself with an almost odorless body spray, but he'd never noticed Martuska wearing anything other than her own natural fragrance. Even if the green-eyed slave girl had access to perfumes or cosmetics, he couldn't imagine what potion could have improved on what nature had already provided.

Martuska spoke for the first time. "How long will Alex have to recover?"

"An hour?" Mistress Dominique said. "Does that seem fair?"

"As long as it's no more than that," Madam Fen replied. "I am eager to settle this." She paused and slowly licked her lips.

The same gesture from Martuska would have been sexy. With Madam Fen, it seemed cruel. Predatory, cat-like. Her lips were blood-red. Alex felt a chill.

Mistress Dominique ushered them into her sleeping chamber, then ordered him to undress and lie on the bed. "Shall we tie him down?"

Madam Fen nodded. "Why not?"

Moments later, he found himself spread-eagled across the bed frame, securely bound by his ankles and wrists. A bottle of lube was placed close at hand on a bedside table. Mistress Dominique reached between his legs, and he heard the chastity device click as it recognized her fingerprint. Sticky precum had already oozed inside the cage; the steel caught for a moment but then slid free.

Alex stared down at himself, willing his penis to relax, not to get hard, but it was no use. His treacherous cock surged to life. Madam Fen hadn't even touched it yet, but her glance struck him so powerfully that he wondered if he might come from that alone.

Thankfully, he didn't.

She perched next to him on the bed, taking care not to touch him since that would start the timer. Slowly, she took the bottle and drizzled a little oil, then rubbed both hands together, working the lubricant into her palms and around her fingers. A second squeeze of the bottle, a second application of its contents, even more thorough than the first.

Then she reached for him.

Mistress Dominique's stopwatch clicked into action.

The cool shock of the cat-woman's touch after so long inside the cage, almost made him cum there and then. He controlled himself with a groan.

"It would be better for you," she murmured, "if you surrendered now. That way, the years you are to spend serving in my household might be a little less difficult."

She squeezed his cock in the slick, oily circle of her forefinger and thumb, ran it up toward the head and then down toward the base, twisting as she went. Alex moaned from the intensity of the unwanted stimulation. Madam Fen might have a reputation for cruelty but she knew how to grant pleasure, too…

Her hand moved again, circled again, pressed again. "But perhaps you look forward to difficulties? Perhaps you fear earning too much of my favor if you co-operate?"

She never stopped the movement of her strong, oiled fingers, squeezing, relaxing, circling, caressing. "I promise you I will never treat you gently."

Alex couldn't last much longer.

"I have many whipping-boys and several exquisitely-painted, barefoot slave girls."

Her left hand moved between his thighs, cupped his hairless scrotum. Captured his balls with oiled fingers. Pressed them. Massaged them. Threatened them.

"Slave girls I sometimes permit to watch as I torture my boys…"

Her right hand continued to work him.

"…until one fragrant beauty pleads for me to show mercy, while another begs to participate…"

Alex did everything he could to resist the rising tide of pleasure. He tried to send his mind somewhere else, anywhere else, but it was useless.

"Imagine what my fragile silken flowers will make of *you*."

He felt his orgasm beginning to build, heard the groan that was his final, hopeless attempt to hold out for a few moments more, and then it was too late. He was past the point of no return and the dark inevitability overwhelmed him so completely that the next sensation of which he was fully aware came from the rapidly-cooling jizz that puddled on his naked belly and trickled down his flank.

"Thirty four seconds," Mistress Dominique remarked. "Not a bad time at all."

Madam Fen's voice was a snarl. "He retains a large element of free will. A properly-broken slave would have ejaculated as soon as his Mistress required it."

"I don't recall saying I required it." Mistress Dominique's tone was conciliatory even as she corrected her guest. "But perhaps this one isn't suitable to your needs after all? I can offer true masochists, natural slaves who would welcome the kind of discipline you offer."

"More boys like Jasper?" Madam Fen asked bitterly. "He is as blank as a roll of *Xuan* paper."

Martuska spoke. "Paper needs to be blank if you wish to cover it exclusively with your own beautiful brush strokes."

"Whip strokes," Madam Fen growled.

Martuska nodded. "Whip strokes, then. Nevertheless, there is surely a place in the world for a scroll that already contains a poem?"

"And how many slaves do *you* own?" Madam Fen asked scornfully.

Martuska's gaze flicked toward Alex. "One," she said.

*

Martuska asked to shower in the small bathroom that adjoined the dungeon's sleeping chamber. Mistress Dominique showed her where to find toiletries, hair-dryer and other requisites.

Alex was permitted to shower next. He took the opportunity to drink his fill from the faucet, in the hope that his bladder would be encouragingly full when the time came. He knew from experience that that would make him as sensitive as possible. Even so, he had no hope at all of returning to anything like his previous hair-trigger level of arousal.

Still naked, he padded back into the bedroom and lay on the bed again.

"I'd like his hands tied to the headboard," Martuska said. "Tightly, if you please. Hurt him a little."

"And his legs?" Mistress Dominique asked.

"Please leave them free."

Once he was securely trussed, Martuska climbed onto the bed next to him. Her long hair was loosely gathered and pinned; she'd dressed herself in the same costume as before. Alex wondered if she'd graze him with her stiletto tips — and if so, would Mistress Dominique count it as a beginning and click the button of her stopwatch?

Fortunately, there was no need for anyone to ask that question, because Martuska knew exactly what she was doing. She arranged her limbs with slow, exquisite precision, swinging one long leg across his body so that she straddled him without touching him at any point. She spread her thighs, arched her back, planted her hands on either side of him. Then she began to crawl up the bed.

Just watching her move was making him hard again.

"The slave should have been blindfolded." Madam Fen's tone was critical, but also held a grudging note of admiration.

Not many Mistresses would have been athletic enough to offer such a rigorously-controlled performance, or lissome enough to make it look so effortless.

Martuska paused near the top of the bed and raised her short leather skirt. Alex saw nothing underneath except for stocking tops and garter straps and sweet flesh. Except for the lightest shadow of downy golden hair, her pussy was perfectly naked.

She was a Mistress now. In his heart he knew that she was *his* Mistress.

Martuska brought her pussy close to his face. He resisted the urge to do what he needed to do, which was to strain upward with extended tongue in the hope she'd permit him to taste it, to lick it. Instead he lay back and simply gazed up.

His cock was fully erect.

"Once I've claimed you," she murmured, "I mean to take you through into the dungeon. I mean to keep you naked, and watch you choose the new collar that will be my token of ownership."

Martuska straightened herself, rising up on her knees and arching her back even more. Alex gazed up at her flesh peeping from behind corset lacings, her slim arms, her hands reaching for the pins that held her hair.

She pulled those pins away and her still-damp locks tumbled free.

Martuska lowered her head a little and swung it from side to side, so that her golden tresses almost brushed Alex's face. So close that he felt the breeze on his cheek, smelled the familiar fragrance of his beloved girl.

"Then I shall whip you, so we can establish from the beginning how our relationship is going to be."

She straightened up, flicked her hair back, and moved down his body.

"And then, once I decide you've earned it, you'll show me what you can do for my pussy with your mouth."

Her skirt was still rucked up around her hips. He could see the sweet naked mound she'd promised him, like a perfect peach, framed by the creases of her toned thighs, by silken garter straps and stocking tops.

"But first, I want you to come."

She reached down and took hold of his erect cock, guided it into her body as she lowered herself onto him.

The pleasure of being inside her tight, wet pussy was like an explosion.

"Come for me!" she commanded and stooped to offer him her long hair again, except this time, she lowered those blonde strands fully to his face, trailed them across him, then drew back to flick him harder, as if she meant to form her locks into some soft, fragrant cat-o'-nine-tails.

Alex lost control completely; if he hadn't been tied down he might have surged up from the mattress to pinion her instead. Martuska raised herself immediately, so that the other two women would not be able to deny the glistening rope of ejaculate that trailed from her pussy, or the gouts that still spurted from Alex's quivering cock as his Mistress's hand continued to pump him up and down.

"Six seconds," Mistress Dominique said. "Impressive indeed."

Madam Fen tossed her head and left without a word.

"She'll be alright," Mistress Dominique said. She glanced at Martuska. "As for you, I suppose you scented your hair?"

"Did I?" Martuska said and smiled.

Mistress Dominique walked towards the doorway. "Feel free to take any remaining scent. It's not as if it will work on anyone else." Her voice faded down the corridor. "Take your time. You earned it."

Martuska released Alex and led him back into the torture chamber where she proceeded to fulfil each and every promise she'd made.

Epilogue

Martuska said goodbye to Dominique in the latter's office. She'd been there before, of course, in order to clean or to run errands, but now she was present as an equal.

She'd been named as the partner in charge of the bank's fledgling Eastern European branch. Her background and language skills made her the obvious choice but Dominique promised her that there was more to the appointment than that. Martuska, she said, was the right woman for the job. No way would the bank risk sending anyone less.

A promising option had become available: a parcel of land, left over after the re-shaping of Eastern Europe around the end of the twentieth century: inaccessible, unclaimed and apparently unwanted. With determination and resources it might be possible to set up not just a bank run by powerful women exercising control over obedient men, but a reasonably-sized city-state.

"We need to get the leaders of the surrounding countries on board," Dominique said. "So they'll sign treaties recognizing our status there."

"Are they men or women?"

"Does it matter?"

Martuska shrugged. "Not really. We know how to deal with either."

"Precisely. I've already invited several of the female politicians and opinion leaders here. As for the males, we've determined that enough of them will be amenable to what we can offer. Several are already being tried out with different scent formulations." She paused and picked up another folder. "Then there's this."

"What is it?"

"Many of the guests enjoy writing reports on the slave boys they entertain. Observations, suggestions, that sort of thing. Some new Mistresses like to use them as a kind of owner's manual to help get the best out of their slaves." She slid the sheaf across the desk. "These are Alex's."

Martuska took the bundle, weighed it in her hand, then set it down again.

"I don't think I'll be needing this," she said.

More Information

This erotic novella grew from the *Femdom Fantasy Whisper Training* audiobook series:

The Audition
Slave Girl in Disgrace
Slave Girl in Torment

www.velluminous.com/LucyFairbourne/